LIGHTS CAMERA DISASTER

LIGHTS CAMERA DISASTER

Erin Dionne

Arthur A. Levine Books

An Imprint of Scholastic Inc.

Library of Congress Cataloging-in-Publication Data available

ISBN 978-1-338-13408-7

10 9 8 7 6 5 4 3 2 1   18 19 20 21 22

Printed in the U.S.A.   23

First edition, April 2018

Book design by Mary Claire Cruz

FOR CHRISTINE C., ANTHONY C., ASHLEIGH M., HAYLEY P., DANIELLE R., ERICA R., DINO T., LUA T., AND ALL OF THE OTHER STUDENTS AT MONTSERRAT COLLEGE OF ART.

RIGHT NOW

I might puke.

Panic ants swarm my body. I can't sit here.

What if no one gets it? Will they boo me?

I scoot out of my row.

"Where are you going?" Zada asks as I pass her.

"Nervous," I mumble. I stand by the emergency exit door. A light breeze blows in around the frame. I breathe. Keep breathing.

"Hester? Is that you?"

Ms. Walker. She's leaning against the wall, a dim shape in the crowded auditorium.

"Hi."

"Did you . . . ?" She gestures at the screen.

My heart hammers, but I stand up straighter. "I did." I can't see her face clearly in the low light, but I'm sure she's frowning. My hands twist together.

The projector comes to life and the soft guitar builds through the overly loud speakers, and the title slides in from the top of the screen:

THIS IS WHO WE ARE

It's my movie. On a big screen.
I might puke, after all.

<< PAUSE >>

How did I get here?
It's kind of a long story. Let's—

<< REWIND >>

- Throwing away the orange
- Mom and Dad in the office
- Hiding in the closet, crying
- Ms. Walker frowning, handing me the test
- My blue elbow
- Reading the MK Nightshade website
- Watching *Jaws*
- Stressing about—

<< STOP >>

<< PLAY >>

FIVE WEEKS AGO

FRIDAY

Ms. Walker stops at my desk, puts my vocab test facedown. Disappointment flows from her pores.

Crud.

I don't want to turn it over. My palms go clammy.

I breathe. I count. I breathe and count.

I'm sweating.

Ms. Walker finishes passing out the tests, returns to the front of the room.

"You may look," she says crisply.

I don't snatch my test like everyone else. The shadow of green marker shows through its last page. Ms. Walker doesn't believe in using red ink because she says it makes tests look "too angry."

"Your homework tonight is to correct your test. Use your dictionary and look up the answers . . ."

In front of me, Sarah high-fives Nirmal across the aisle. No homework for them.

Meanwhile, my heart gets heavier with each beat. I slowly slide the test packet across the desk, pick it up by its corner, and peel it back.

If this were a movie, I'd turn it over and it'd be an A. I'd be shocked, surprised, but secretly have known I could do it. Maybe there'd be a dance sequence, where the room would go dark and I'd jump out of my chair and do solo spins and leap onto the desks to a cheesy pop soundtrack.

But this is not a movie. At the top, in a big circle, is a D+. Next to it, *Better—but not good enough* is spelled out in Ms. W.'s perfect green printing.

My chest locks, like my ribs won't expand and my heart won't go and I can't get any air in. Then my heart slams, hard, pounding like I'm running for my life.

An anxiety attack. I've had them before, but not in the middle of a class. My hands shake and my skin gets tingly-itchy-twitchy, like there are ants swarming over me, and I want to pull. Them. OFF.

Pop out of my chair. Can't remember my calming strategies. Can barely remember my *name.*

Bolt up the row. My foot catches in the strap of my messenger bag, yanks it across the floor, and all my stuff spills out. Can't even look. Just GO.

The room is silent.

Bang into the classroom door, scrabble for the knob, throw it open. Behind me, Ms. Walker calls out, but her words blur and mash together.

Stagger-run out into the hall, find my feet, pound past some lockers. I'm a gazelle chased by a lion in a nature documentary.

Classroom doors, signs, and flyer blow by and I'm in front of Mr. Sinclair, the special ed counselor's office, heart still slamming.

Don't knock, don't stop, just throw the door open. A girl wearing a royal blue headscarf sits wide-eyed in the squashy red guest chair.

Mr. Sinclair takes one look at me and tells the girl to leave. She bolts past me like *I'm* the lion.

"Hess! Hester! Slow it down! You are in charge!" Mr. S. says, and nudges me toward the chair. I sink, struggling to bring my uncontrollable gasps to a more reasonable, human-being breathing speed. Inhaling as fast as a hummingbird isn't working for me. My vision blurs. Limbs shake. It's hard to swallow. Spit pools in my mouth.

"You're hyperventilating," he says. I manage a weak nod.

"Head down!" he orders. I drop my head to my knees.

"Can I put my hand on your back?" he asks, and I nod.

His big hand rests, solid and warm. It grounds me. He counts, "One-two-three-in, one-two-three-out," and after a minute or so I'm actually able to follow his directions. The shaking subsides. The panic ants retreat. I'm breathing.

The bell rings.

"What happened?" he asks, after it's clear that I've mostly rejoined the world of the functional.

I shrug, helpless. "Vocab test returned," I say, using short sentences like he told me, so I won't talk too fast and get worked up. "I got a D plus." Breath. "It's not good enough." Two breaths. "I'm not going to be able to do the Hoot."

Mr. Sinclair kneels on the rug in front of me.

"What's our strategy here?" he asks.

I shake my head. There are no thoughts or strategies in my brain. Only a big red STOP sign, blocking everything.

"The one-inch frame," he says. He leans over to his desk and picks up a small empty picture frame. "Focus on one thing at a time."

This I can do.

"The vocab test," he prompts.

I nod. Breathe. "I got a D plus."

"How did you do on the last one?"

"I failed," I admit, seeing where he's going with this. "But it's not enough!" I say, louder than I'd intended. On the wall across from me is a poster of a dog completely covered in mud. The caption: *It washes off.* Yeah, right. I hate that picture.

I breathe again.

"You feel like you're trying and it's not enough?" Mr. Sinclair says. His bald spot shines in the light.

I nod, miserable. "She even said so on my test."

"You *are* improving," he says. "You have to keep doing the work, Hess." He has this expression on his face—I'm not sure what you call it, but it's friendly and serious and thoughtful and kind of stern, all at once.

I guess I'd know that word if I'd passed my vocab test.

"One thing at a time," he says.

He keeps going, telling me I am okay, and everything will be fine, and blah blah blah. And part of me wants to believe him.

Part of me really does.

But the other part? That part thinks nothing is going to be fine at all.

FRIDAY LUNCH

"Took long enough," Max says as I step out of Mr. Sinclair's office. But he grins while he says it. He and Nev are leaning up against the lockers across the hall. It's lunchtime. Max hands me my messenger bag and I glance inside.

"Camera's there," Nev says. I'm grateful that she looks out for me, even though I drive her nuts sometimes. She's super-organized and a planner, and I am so not. She's also the one who pulled our little group together—she and Max met in Theater Club last year, after he switched into our school when his family moved here. Like Nev, he's more into books and theater than sports, and they bonded over some musical about a president and an elementary school obsession with the Wings of Fire series. I could care less about either, so I spent a lot of time bored when the three of us were together. But then I found out that Max was actually in a chicken nugget commercial as a little kid and is totally into acting—and that's when we formed our movie production group.

Nev and Max are my actors. I do scripts and shooting. We're not a formal club or anything, we just work on our movies outside of school (or *movie*—we haven't actually finished one yet). Nev is super busy and tries a different club every quarter, but always does theater to keep up with her skills. She's also doing Hook and Line right now—the crochet club. Or knitting. I can't remember. It has yarn. She talked me into doing Movie Club last year, but this year my grades don't meet the minimum for activity participation. No big loss—Movie Club was lame. The kid who runs it has no idea what makes a good movie. I mean, he thinks *The Last Airbender* is the best movie ever made. And he likes the *Star Wars* prequels better than the originals. Oh, please.

"Thanks, guys," I say. "Panic attack."

"About . . . ?" Nev asks.

I don't answer. I want to talk about something else.

"You nearly gave *me* a panic attack," Max says as we make our way to the caf. "You bolted past the door of my math class like you were trying to outrun a tornado."

I am a tornado, I think.

"Sorry! It was scary on my end of it, too. Oh—I have a new scene for you guys to look at," I say.

"Finally!" Nev says.

We sit at our table in the corner and I dig through my bag for the script pages I stuffed in there last night. We're making a short spy movie for the school talent show—the Howard Hoffer Junior High Talent Night, aka the Hoot. So we have to finish it. This will be the first time I show a movie on a big screen, like a real director. Nev is a secret agent assigned to go back to junior high to find a teacher who is planning Mass Destruction Of Some Kind (I need to work that part out). Max works for the evil teacher, trying to stop Nev before she ruins their plans.

While they pore over the script, instead of opening my lunch, I power up my camera and point it at the two worried-looking sixth graders perched at the other end of our table, staring at their cafeteria-gray burgers and fries. The starchy smell of the fries fills the caf. The last of the adrenaline leaves my body. Seeing things through a lens makes me calm, gives me control.

"Lasagna? Really?" Max says. He stuffs almost half his sandwich into his mouth while he reads.

INTERIOR. Noisy, busy middle school cafeteria.

AGENT SATCHEL stands at the edge of the room holding a lunch tray of lasagna, looking for a place to sit. MAXIMUM EVIL approaches, with a lunch bag.

MAXIMUM EVIL
Do you need somewhere to sit?

AGENT SATCHEL
(nods)

MAXIMUM EVIL
Follow me.

Camera follows the two of them. MAXIMUM EVIL leads her out of the cafeteria.

AGENT SATCHEL
(suspicious)
Aren't we supposed to eat in there?

MAXIMUM EVIL
(over his shoulder)
I have a better spot.

INT. Door to Room 225. AGENT SATCHEL knows what's behind that door. Her cover is blown.

AGENT SATCHEL
Hey!

MAXIMUM EVIL turns. AGENT SATCHEL tosses her lunch tray of lasagna right at his face. Takes off down the hall, trying to get to the main office.

MAXIMUM EVIL wipes his face, runs after her. Chase ensues. AGENT SATCHEL throws hall garbage cans in his path.

"We need to talk about this," Max says through a mouth full of sandwich.

"One sec." I pan the room one more time, then shut down the camera. If I use this, I'll have to edit out the roar of kids talking, trays smacking the tables, and chairs scraping the floor. Worth it? "What's up?"

"How are we going to shoot it?" Max asks.

"Do you like it?"

"Totally." Nev jumps in. "But it's a good question. We're going to run from the cafeteria, and I'm throwing stuff in the hall? How is that even possible?"

I thought they'd be all excited. "We'll figure it out," I mumble.

"Maybe we can get permission?" Max offers.

Nev snickers. "Doubt it." The two of them go back and forth on whether or not the vice principal will let us if we ask. But every spy movie needs a chase scene, so we'll make it happen.

The bell rings, and I glance at my still-unopened Avengers lunchbox. My stomach growls. I didn't get to eat, but talking about the script distracted Nev and Max from more conversation about my panic attack. Who wants to relive that? Not me.

They pack up their lunches and I stuff my camera in my bag. I also grab half of my PB&J and take a giant bite as we step away from the table.

Nev catches me and glares. Our school has rules about where we can eat peanut butter because of the kids with nut allergies.

I sigh, toss the sandwich, rinse and spit into the garbage can, and stick my tongue out at Nev. No more Skippy. Hopefully next period I won't kill anyone with my breath.

"Are you okay?" Nev asks as we head down to the science wing.

I shrug. Not really, but what is there to say? She's listened to me stress about my grades forever. She's over it. I'm over it.

"Maybe you can ask Walker for extra credit?"

"Yeah, right. You know her deal. No way." We dodge a group of kids.

Nev fiddles with the end of her long braid.

"Well, maybe . . . since the Hoot is coming, you could ask her anyway? My class is doing that author assignment, where you write to your favorite author. It's so easy, you could do that."

But I'm not in the advanced class.

I don't have a favorite author.

I don't read if I can help it.

I don't say anything.

"I picked Megan Marie—she wrote that book about selkies that I loved . . ." Nev goes on as we make our way into the classroom. "I mean, I think you should. Try. Maybe Mr. Sinclair could help convince her. 'Cause if your marking period grades aren't good . . ." She trails off, which is fine, because I don't want her to finish.

She doesn't need to, because inside I'm screaming, *I know! If I fail, there's no movie in the Hoot.*

⋘ FAST-FORWARD ⋙

- Boring rest of the day
- Pizza for dinner!
- Stay up late and watch Alfred Hitchcock marathon on AMC
- Sleep in

⋘ RESUME PLAY ⋙

SATURDAY

"They are so dead," Max whispers. He peeks out from between his fingers. "So—"

"Shhh!" Nev shushes him without looking away from the TV. "Watch!"

The boat, helpless without a motor, bobs on the surface of the water. The camera pulls back—way back, the boat is small in the frame—and *pop!* The yellow barrel dotted with the blinking orange light pops to the surface.

Max jumps. I whack him with a pillow.

"This is the best part!"

The shark goes for the ship, and we all yell when it rams the back and tears off a piece of the boat.

Nev hops onto the couch from the floor. We push into the cushions, into one another. The shark circles back—

The lights flick on.

"You kids need a snack or anything?" Nev's mom calls.

"MA!" Nev shouts. "No! You're ruining the movie!" The lights go off.

Crunch.

"Quint-kebob!" says Max. But when the shark clamps down on Quint's body, Max goes quiet.

Chief Brody does his thing with the oxygen tank, and it's buh-bye shark. As Brody and Hooper paddle back to shore, Max resumes his never-ending movie chatter.

"That was awesome!" He bounces on the couch cushions. "I mean, I heard it was good, but it was, like, way better than I expected." Nev whomps him with a fuzzy pink throw pillow.

"You were totally scared," she teases.

"Was not!"

"Was too!"

I grin and slip my camera out to record their show. Neither of them were interested in watching *Jaws*, but it was my pick—we take turns, otherwise we'd never agree on anything—so they had to go along with it once I got here. I was late.

I'm just about to press RECORD when Max catches me.

"Hey!" He chucks the pink pillow in my direction. I duck and it flies by.

"Rule breaker!" Nev yells.

"All right, all right," I grumble, putting the camera back in its case. That's also part of the rule of Movie Extravaganza: no camera. I'm bummed that they caught me, but the moment is wrecked now, anyway.

Max flops back on the couch. "Anyone want those snacks? I'm hungry."

"You're always hungry," Nev points out. But she bounces up and leads us upstairs.

There's a bowl of cashews on the counter, and I dive in. Nev rummages in a cupboard and pulls out a bag of chips and salsa. Max grabs the jar and holds the label next to his cheek.

"Olé! Olé! Olé!" he sings. "There's nothing greater to eat today!" He waits, eyes wide, as Nev and I exchange glances. Max knows every food commercial on TV, plus he writes them in his spare time and is convinced that's how he'll make his millions.

"Olé salsa, try it and you'll buy it?" he adds, hopeful. We shake our heads.

"No," Nev says.

"Come on!"

"Keep trying," Nev says. She takes the jar from him, and it makes a hissing crack as she opens it—and it brings her mom straight to the kitchen. She's wearing blue running pants and a hoodie, which is a surprise. When I see her during the week, she's usually in a suit. Most of the time we're at Nev's dad's or my house on the weekend.

"We have an open jar in the fridge," she says.

"Sorry," Nev says, and rolls her eyes at me when her mom's not looking. Nev gets a bowl and pours the chips in. Max grabs a handful. Her mom shakes her head.

"You guys finish watching your movie?" Mouths stuffed, we make noises that mean "yes."

"Max isn't going to go swimming for a long time," I add. He scowls at me.

"I was not scared," he says for the thousandth time.

"I was," Nev's mom says. She leans over the counter and dips a chip into the salsa. "I remember watching that movie with a bunch of girlfriends right before going to the beach for the Fourth of July. I don't think we went into the water at all!" She laughs. "That movie's been scaring people for ages, mostly because of an accident."

"Whup?" My mouth is full of tangy salsa and chips, and crumbs spray everywhere. I swallow and try again. "What?"

"I'd have thought you knew this, Hess." She looks kind of pleased with herself that I don't. "The mechanical shark they called Bruce kept breaking down. So Spielberg had to shoot around it. That's why you don't actually see the shark very much." She chomps a chip. "Makes it scarier, when it's left up to your imagination, don't you think?"

I mull this over while Nev and Max argue over what is scarier: seeing something or not seeing it. I don't even bother to get involved, because, like Spielberg, I know the imagination is way scarier than what anyone puts on film. All the great directors knew that. Alfred Hitchcock kept lots of stuff offscreen—like when Janet Leigh dies in *Psycho*. He never actually shows her getting stabbed in the movie.

Mentally, I flip through *The Spy Who Bugged Me* footage. How can I shoot the chase scene so we can make it work and not get in trouble?

"Earth to Hess!" Nev's fingers snap in front of my face. "Earth to Hess!"

I close my eyes for a sec, clearing the image from my head and trying to focus. "Yeah?"

"We're taking the chips downstairs. Coming?"

"Olé." I trail behind them, working on my options.

FOUR WEEKS AGO

‹‹ FAST-FORWARD ››

- Boring Sunday
- Boring day at school Monday
- Recording my brother, Jack, in his bedroom
- He gets angry
- I go to my room
- There's a NOISE

‹‹ RESUME PLAY ››

MONDAY EVENING

The loud crack makes me stop working in my video editing program. "What the . . . ?"

Then Dad's voice, sounding not good at all—hoarse and awful—"Bonnieeee!" He draws out Mom's name in a way I've never heard before.

A sick sensation fills my body and turns my stomach to pudding. I push back from my desk and race downstairs at the same time as Jack and Mom. We meet in the kitchen, and I'm guessing my eyes look as big and wild as theirs.

"Where is he?" Mom peers down the basement stairs.

"Bonnie!" Dad calls again, and now we can tell he's at the front of the house.

Track-star Jack gets there first. He throws open the door and there's Dad in his running gear, curled at the bottom of the front stairs. There's blood on his head, but it's like he doesn't even care about that, because he's clutching his right shoulder with his left arm. His face is gray and knotted with pain.

The loose flagstone—one he keeps saying he's going to fix—is in pieces around him.

We stand frozen, staring. Mom, of course, snaps to action first.

"Call an ambulance!" she directs. I have no idea where my phone is. I'm shaking and couldn't dial if I wanted to. Jack pushes past me into the house. I back up, bumping my head against our mailbox, a tide of panic rising in me. Mom crouches next to Dad, trying to see how badly he's hurt.

"Get a towel or washcloth!" she snaps. "And ice!"

I jerk forward and stand up, heart hammering somewhere in my throat. My legs and arms don't want to obey. I fumble with the doorknob and barrel into the house, nearly tripping over my own feet.

In the kitchen, I grab a clean dish towel. My heart slams. Jack's hanging on to the edge of the table with one hand, knuckles white. He's giving our address to the operator.

"I don't know," he says. "I'm inside." It's like he's forgotten that he can walk and talk on a cell phone.

I'm no better. Should I wet the cloth or bring it dry? In the movies, head wounds are serious. Will Dad bleed to death on the front lawn? I can't decide what to do.

"Hess-TER!" Mom roars from outside, and I rush back to her with the towel, almost falling down the steps myself. I crouch next to them.

"Be careful. We don't need you hurt, too," Mom says. She sees what I brought.

"No ice?" she says. She must see the sinking feeling in my gut right on my face, because she sighs, then folds the towel into a small square and holds it onto Dad's head. He's sitting up now, at least, leaning against the step. Blood soaks the right side of his shirt.

"Jack's on the phone," I gasp through my tiny windpipe. Breathe.

Breathe. Breathe. The panic ants swarm me and I stand up. "Is he okay? His head . . ." I don't even know what to say. My hands twist together, fingers digging at skin.

Dad's head is back, nearly resting on the step behind him. His left hand crosses his body. And then I notice—his right shoulder doesn't look right. It's . . . lower somehow. My stomach gives a slow roll.

The towel is nearly soaked through. *Where is Jack? Where is the ambulance?*

"I think it's broken," Dad says, his face a bloodless white. And then we hear the sirens.

TUESDAY

Mom and I are arguing over my language arts assignment.

Or, where my language arts assignment *is.*

"I gave you the folders. I labeled them. I *put them in your bag.*" Mom's frustration is approaching orange alert status. She rubs the bridge of her nose under her glasses, eyes closed. Dark circles from our late night at the hospital ring her eyes.

"I don't know what happened to it," I say for the thousandth time, the words splatting lamely on the table. "I put it in the folder."

Mom opens her eyes. "Which folder?" she says through gritted teeth, "because we've looked through all of them and I don't see it anywhere. Do you?"

A ball of misery rolls in my stomach. I *want* to remember. I want to put the language arts stuff in the blue folder, and math in the red one, and social studies in green (even though science should totally be green, right?), and whatever goes in the purple one in that one, but when teachers start handing papers out, it's like my brain flattens and all the folders are the wrong one. So I put it in whichever one I grab, no matter what it says on the white sticky label Mom put on the front. Mr. Sinclair calls it "executive function disorder," which sounds to me like a disease where you can't execute someone, but really means that you can't organize. Or plan stuff. Or manage time. Or switch focus.

In sixth grade, when I was tested and we found out I had it, it made everything clearer: Now we knew why I couldn't find my worksheets, and why my locker was a mess, and why I kept confusing the homework assignments. But knowing why something happens doesn't make it stop happening. Or make you less frustrated by it. That's what Mr. Sinclair's strategies are for.

"I tried to put it in the right one," I whisper.

My mom looks like she wants to execute someone right now. Her face is red and her eyes bug out a little. Even her normally smooth bobbed haircut is going flyaway frizzy. And it's my fault.

It usually is.

Although she's been way more patient with me since we found out about the EFD—she's a super-organized person who never could understand why I was such a hot mess—we still struggle over my homework.

Sometimes the strategies just aren't enough.

She puffs air from between her lips.

"I need a minute," she says, and pushes back from the table. She's probably going to sit on the now broken front steps, which is what she does when we drive her crazy.

In front of me, homework and graded papers march across the table in a neat row. Grids and lines are supposed to help me, but today the pages turn into white walls and the space between becomes a maze.

My hands itch. I want the camera. Mom makes me put it on

top of the fridge so I'll focus on my work, but with it there and her not here, all I want to do is shoot. I set up the frame in my head:

INT. Close-up of a tabletop. Stacks of paper line its perfect surface. The camera closes in on one, blurry words coming into focus: a test.

Hess Greene   Language Arts, Ms. Walker

Weekly Reading Comprehension Quiz #2: THE GIVER

A big green D with a sad face inside is circled on the top. "Did you read?" written next to it.

Of course I hadn't read it. I'd watched the movie. Most of my language arts tests—and we take a *lot* of tests in Ms. Walker's class—are marked with frowny faces. My other teachers let me do cool extra credit projects, like making videos, when my grades slip into frowny face range. I am so bummed I got Ms. W. instead of Mrs. Hoffstedder, who retired at the end of last year and who let kids do all kinds of interesting projects. There's nothing interesting this year. Only things I stink at. Over and over again.

I'm already taking summer school for social studies and math. The district only lets kids take two summer classes—which I also did after sixth and seventh grades, even with tutoring and extra help.

I hoped this year would be different, and it is—it's harder. During the winter, failing felt far away, but now that it's April I'm freaking out a little. I've never failed three classes before. What could happen?

One thing is for sure: If I can't get it together, there won't be a movie in the Hoot. I'll fail my friends, too.

If this were a movie, I could pull everything off in a way that would make the audience cheer for me.

But this is not a movie. I can't even pull out the right folder. I drop my forehead to the table and close my eyes. There's a heaviness around my heart.

Mom returns. I lift my head. That heaviness? It's the weight of disappointing my parents. Over and over again.

"I'm sorry," I whisper.

"I know, honey," she says. Her face is smoother, teeth not clenched. "Let's try again."

A breath.

"Did you write the assignment in your planner?"

My planner?

I sigh. "It's probably in a galaxy far, far away . . ."

«« PAUSE »»

You want to know why I'm so into movies?

I've always loved sitting in a theater as it gets dark, watching the story unfold on the big screen like I'm peeking in a window into another world. But I didn't want to *make* movies until this one time I was out with Mom and Jack when I was eight. We saw *The Avengers* and the credits started to roll and Mom and I stood up.

"Sit down," Jack whispered at us. "Don't go yet."

"But it's over!" I said to him. "I want to get ice cream!" Mom had promised us ice cream after.

"Watch," he said. "You'll see."

What I thought he wanted me to see were the rows and rows of names that scrolled by on the screen. I was annoyed at first, then curious.

"Key grip? Best boy? Director's assistant?" Who were those people? What did they do? How did their names get up there?

What Jack really wanted to see was the credit cookie at the end—end of the movie, after the credits: a short skit with Iron Man and the other Avengers. It was funny and quick and cracked all of us up.

That was the first time I'd seen a credit cookie and I was full of questions. The big one:

"They can do that?" I asked him as we walked across the parking lot, lagging behind Mom. "They can stick a mini-movie on the end of the big movie?"

"They can do whatever they want," he answered.

I thought about that: Getting to tell the story however you want seemed so cool. It was way better than my eight-year-old life, when everyone was telling me to do *something* all the time. But—

"Who're they, anyway?"

"The producers. The directors. They're the ones who make all the decisions about the movie," he told me. "The actors do what they say, and then the director takes all of the stuff he shot and puts it together to tell the story."

"Well then, that's what I'm going to be."

Jack really had no clue what directors did, but his bad description was enough to get me to pay attention to who directed every movie I saw after that day, and to ask for a camera for my birthday when I was ten.

People still tell me to do stuff all the time, but now I get to tell stories any way I want.

« RESUME PLAY »

TUESDAY NIGHT

After that bad scene with Mom, I am determined to fix things. I will ask Ms. Walker to let me do extra credit. I will focus as hard as I can on my classes. I will get our movie in the Hoot.

Sweeping the papers, old copies of *Movie Weekly Magazine*, and random granola bar wrappers that cover the top of my desk into a pile, I put them on the floor. I dig my notebook out of my backpack and sit down. Then I push back from the chair, grab my camera off my bed, and run to my parents' bedroom, where I knock. Dad grunts, and I stick my head in.

He's propped up in bed, watching *Star Trek: The Next Generation* reruns. I stand for a few minutes, watching the crew of the Enterprise fight the latest threat, then I remember what I'm doing there.

"Can you watch this for me?" Without waiting for an answer, I leave the camera on a shelf near the door, and bolt back up to my room.

I open my spiral notebook to a fresh page:

Dear Ms. Walker, I write. *I would like to propose a special project and I'm hoping you'll consider it. . . .*

I force my attention to stay on the notebook. Chain it there, with heavy ropes and locks and threats.

And I write her a dang letter.

WEDNESDAY

In the morning I wave my envelope in Nev's and Max's faces on our way to the lockers.

"What's that?" Max says through a mouthful of cinnamon raisin bagel. He crams another huge piece between his teeth. There's cream cheese smeared on his cheek and his hoodie is on inside out. We stop at his locker first.

"A letter," I say, unable to contain my smug grin. Max pulls out his books, the rest of his bagel clamped between his teeth.

"Duh," Nev says. "Who's it to?"

"Ms. W.," I answer. "Asking if I can make a video for an extra credit project."

"A video?" Nev tilts her head. "Another one?"

I don't know what she means. "Like you suggested the other day. To make sure my grades stay up for the Hoot. Academic permission slips are due the Monday after next."

A slow, crumb-covered grin spreads across Max's face and he swings his locker shut. "So you think that a letter will be more convincing than just asking? Smooooth."

Nev frowns. "It seems like that's taking on way more work, Hess."

"It's perfect," I say, ignoring her. "I'm going to take it to Mr. Sinclair and see if he'll help."

Of course, Sarah, the girl who sits in front of me in Walker's class, has the locker next to Max. She stops messing with her books and turns to see what the excitement is about. Last week I heard her going on about this "hilarious" movie that she'd seen — *Bill & Ted's Excellent Adventure*. Um, yeah. It's only been hilarious for almost *thirty years*. Welcome to the world, Sarah.

"What's going on?" she asks, like she hasn't been listening.

"None of your business," I say.

"If it's about our class it's my business." I don't agree with her logic, but before I can say anything else, she plucks the envelope out of my hand and unfolds the letter.

Why hadn't I sealed it?

"Give it back," I demand. "It's for a teacher."

"You want to make a video to your favorite author? For extra credit in *Walker's* class?" Sarah cackles. "Are you serious?! She'll never let you do it."

"I wasn't asking *you*," I say through gritted teeth. I snatch the envelope and letter back, neither of which are as crisp and white as when I folded and packed them this morning.

"Go brush your hair or something," Nev says.

Sarah scowls and stomps away.

My good mood is toast. Sarah's right — there's no way Ms. W. will go for this, with or without Mr. Sinclair backing me up. I stuff the envelope into the front pocket of my backpack and, still doomed, don't say anything else to Nev and Max.

WEDNESDAY MID-MORNING

By the time I go to language arts, some of the pride has come back. At the beginning of the period, while Ms. Walker has us doing some silent reading and before I lose my nerve, I slip up to her desk. Her head is down; she's reading, too — *The Seventh Wish*.

Shyness overcomes me, and I stand quietly, not wanting to bother her and not wanting to go back to my seat. I wish I had spoken with Mr. Sinclair before class, but Sarah's comments had me half convinced not to give her the letter at all. I turn the envelope over and over in my hands. More wrinkles. I try to smooth it on my leg. Maybe I should just sit down and forget this idea.

She looks up.

Too late.

"Hess!" she whispers. "I was so into my book that I didn't see you there." She laughs a little, and I feel better. I hold the envelope out to her. She seems puzzled.

"It's about my grades," I explain.

Her face gets serious. "Renewing your commitment to the class, I hope?"

I dig at my cuticles and remember my dad telling me how much grown-ups appreciate eye contact. I force myself to meet her level, cool eyes. "It's a proposal letter. A pitch."

"A pitch?" Her eyes narrow. Behind me, a few low whispers begin.

"Yeah," I mumble, watching the floor again. "Just . . . read it and let me know what you think, okay? Please," I add, an afterthought.

"Back to your book!" she directs someone behind me. "All right, Hess. But no promises."

"Thank you," I say automatically.

"You may retake your seat and finish your reading." I slink back to my chair. My chances are probably not good. I sigh, and wish again that I'd gone to see Mr. S. as I'd kind of planned.

Unless it's a movie, I only "kind of" plan stuff.

I try to focus on the novel I'm supposed to be reading, but the lines blur together and I end up staring at the same page, not even bothering to turn it. All that runs through my mind is *please let me do it, please let me do it* . . . on endless, pleading repeat. This has to work. It has to save *The Spy Who Bugged Me*.

It has to save our chances for the Hoot.

Ms. Walker calls the class to attention and tells us about our next test on *The Giver*. She writes chapter numbers on the board and I write them down in my planner. But I've missed which day it's going to be on. Hopefully I'll remember to ask Max.

I write *Ask Max about test* in the planner.

Walker keeps going—how she's going to grade it, how many points it's worth, blah blah blah. If I pass the test, and she approves my project, I'll be set. Extra credit could boost my grade for the Hoot, and I could show the whole school our movie on a big screen!

The bell rings, and we pack up.

"Hester," Ms. Walker says, right as I'm passing her. I stop and reverse, like a fish jerked on a line. She's parked behind her desk, still as a fisherman, hands folded on top of my letter. I stand in front of her. And wait.

"How does this qualify as an English assignment?"

I meet her eyes. "I wrote a letter."

"To me."

I nod, staring at my worn black Converse. The tight, panicky feeling grips my chest. Cannot freak out right now. *Cannot.*

I take a deep breath. "Ms. W., it's a really cool project. I can make a video, which needs a script and a shot list and a plan — that's all writing. I can give you copies of that stuff. It's probably way more work than just writing a regular assignment or anything." Inside, I'm crossing everything — fingers, toes, eyes — and trying to calm my racing heart and brain. What if she says no? What do I do then? My friends will be so mad at me. I suck-suck-suck. Outside, I try to stand still. Freeze frame.

If this were a movie, the camera would circle us and the desk. It's a standoff like in a Western. She'd crack a big smile and tell me to go for it.

Instead, the clock hums. Lockers slam in the halls. My stomach growls. I should be at lunch.

Finally, she drops the corners of her mouth into a deep frown.

"I don't like it. I don't offer extra credit, and frankly, I feel as though you're taking advantage." She raises a hand to stop me from responding. "But your letter shows an investment that I haven't seen from you before." She pauses and adjusts the cuff of her sweater.

The tightness around my chest makes it hard to breathe. The panic ants will come out soon. *Stay calm stay calm staycalm.*

"Has Mr. Sinclair approved of this project?"

I don't trust myself to speak, and can't even move my head to shake it no. She waits for a second, and I manage the tiniest head turn ever.

"I see." She frowns again. "Against my better judgment, I'm going to let you do this. You have one week. But—and this is a big condition, Hester—if I feel that this project is taking away from your in-class work, it comes to an end. And I want Mr. Sinclair looped in on this. Understood?"

I exhale in a tiny puff and squeak out a "Thank you!"

"Go to lunch," she says.

I manage not to run until after I get out of the classroom, then I race down the hall toward the caf, outrunning the panic and tightness.

Finally—a chance to do something I'm good at.

Finally—a chance to save my grade.

Finally—a chance to tell my own story.

WEDNESDAY AFTERNOON

Dad's downstairs for the first time since he came home from the hospital late Monday night, and he still doesn't look like himself. He hasn't showered and his hair sticks up like a bad crown. Gray stubble shadows his cheeks and chin, and his eyes are sunken and hollow-looking, even though all he's been doing is sleeping.

He stands in front of the fridge, and leans a little, like he wants to grab the handle with his right hand. A swift hiss of breath, and he awkwardly grabs it lefty.

"Can I get you something?" I want to be helpful, but I'm not sure how. Dad is bent over, peering into the fridge, moving stuff around with his left hand. An open container of yogurt splats onto the floor.

"Of all the—!" he barks. The smell fills the kitchen: peach flavor. "Who leaves open yogurt in the fridge, anyway?"

Mom crushes his pills into it, because they are hard on his stomach. It's probably not a good idea to point that out.

"I'll clean it up," I say. "Don't worry about it."

He sets a jar of jelly on the counter and tries to reach up to open the cabinet with the peanut butter. But even using his good arm makes him cringe.

"I got it," I say. I scoot between him and the counter and pass him the peanut butter, then take two slices of bread out of the bag. I bend and wipe up the yogurt, still holding the bread. Oops. One of the slices is a little squished, so I try to smooth it out on the cutting board.

Meanwhile, Dad's having a hard time getting the peanut butter on the knife, holding the jar against the counter with his stomach and bad hand, scooping with his "good" one.

"Need help?"

He hands the knife and Skippy over. "Thanks. My arm is killing me. I don't know how I'm going to be able to do anything."

I spread extra jelly on, the way he likes it, and finish making the sandwich. "It won't hurt like this forever," I explain. "When I broke my arm it hurt really bad for about four days, and then it was okay." I fell out of a tree in our neighbor's yard three years ago, trying to get their dog on video. Luckily my camera was okay.

"I remember." He kisses the top of my head. "I have more appreciation for what you went through." He pauses, takes a bite of his sandwich. "I have no idea how I'm going to be able to work."

"You'll figure it out," I say, and I offer the only piece of advice I can think of. "When Bruce the shark broke down shooting *Jaws*, Steven Spielberg still got the movie made."

Dad raises an eyebrow at me. "How did he do that?"

"He worked around it," I say.

WEDNESDAY NIGHT

I scour my brother's bookshelves like Indiana Jones searching for the Holy Grail, trying to find a book I've read or an author I recognize so I can get this desperately needed extra credit. My proposal to Ms. Walker was to make a short movie "letter" to my favorite author.

I *have* read books—seriously—I just don't like to. Everything I read goes through me like . . . water. My brain doesn't hold on to words, only pictures:

Obi-Wan being struck down by Darth Vader.

Iron Man standing in the middle of the track, facing Ivan Vanko and the electric whips.

The long line of penguins waddling across a frozen plain toward home.

Hiro's devastated face as he lets go of Baymax.

It's no surprise that my bookshelf holds DVDs, Blu-rays, and a bunch of ancient VHS tapes from my parents' collection, right? Unless it was made into a movie, it evaporates.

I think about making a movie about a girl whose touch makes stuff evaporate. It would start off small . . . a pencil. Her bed. Then . . . her little brother. Her parents. Their house. *The world.* Hmmmm . . . I like it. File it into a mental folder of "potential horror/fantasy/dsytopian stories." I really want to put it in my *actual* ideas folder on the computer so Max, Nev, and I can make it some day, but I need to be productive. Focused on schoolwork. Focused on this extra credit.

I force my attention back to Jack's books.

One of the novels is sticking out from the rest of the ones on the shelf, and the sliver of cover looks familiar even though the jewel green spine doesn't. I tug.

A Sea of Serpents reads the gold script. The image beneath it is taken straight from the movie: a black and green sea serpent wrapped around a wooden boat, the knight, Sir Oakheart, with sword held high, aiming straight for the creature's neck. The boat splinters, the sea is stormy, the sky boils with bruised-looking purple clouds.

I *loved* that movie! I forgot it was based on a book. This small fishing village was tormented by a sea serpent that destroyed their boats, ate their catches, and started consuming the villagers. Only Sir Oakheart, with his sword of heart's blood steel, was able to kill the monster—but he nearly died in the process. *Of course*, a cute village girl has just the herbs needed to cure the serpent venom and saves his life, blah blah blah. The CGI effects with the monster were sick. In IMAX 3-D, every scale dripped perfectly. There were a few things I would've done differently—the romance was predictable, and some of the shots used too much lens flare—but overall the movie was great. One of the best fantasy epics I've seen recently.

Epic is the key word.

The book is short and fat, and the spine has those white lines on it from being opened a ton of times. One of Jack's favorites,

I guess. I flip through the pages—small type, and no pictures, obviously. So much small type.

Would I have to read it?

Maybe I could watch the movie again to make the video?

From downstairs, the door slams. Jack's home from track practice.

I tuck the book under my arm and scoot down the hall to my room.

While I was pilfering Jack's library, Mom left my assignment book open and a to-do list all made out on top of the pile of papers on my bed. She's listed five items under *Wednesday To-Dos*:

Choose an author for extra credit assignment
Social studies questions
Math problems, pages 455–457 (Even? Odd? Text Nev)
Finish coloring acids & bases science worksheet
Spanish quiz review

And she's signed my homework planner for today, tomorrow, and Friday already. *What?!*

According to my school 504 plan, Mom and Dad are supposed to sign my homework planner every night, but I guess Mom is stressed out dealing with Dad. By this late in the year most of my teachers have stopped checking, anyway.

I can totally color the worksheet tomorrow at lunch. And the Spanish quiz isn't until Friday . . . Monday? Whatever. I have time. Social studies and math . . . ugh. I'm taking summer school for those anyway. I choose a blue marker from the tipped-over jar on my desk and draw a thick line through *Choose an author for extra credit assignment.* Then I flop onto my bed—on top of that science worksheet, which wrinkles a little—open the novel, and flip to the beginning.

It doesn't start where the movie begins. Instead, there's this girl in a forest, being stalked by a Thing. But the girl doesn't know Thing is there. It's interesting, but I keep picturing how it went in the movie and I have to reread the paragraphs in order to follow along.

I get through the first chapter and the girl is still alive.

So is Thing.

But I'm toast.

‹‹ FAST-FORWARD ››

- School is boring
- I forget my lunch; Mom brings it, annoyed
- Max still wants to know how we'll shoot the chase scene

‹‹ RESUME PLAY ››

THURSDAY

INT. School lunchroom. Kids laughing, talking loudly, jostling for space at tables and carrying lunch bags and trays.

Zoom in on a table in the corner. Three kids—two girls and a boy—sit, lunches spread. The boy with close-cropped dark hair looks at the camera, mid-bite of a sandwich. Scowls.

MAX
Shut it off, Hess!

End scene.

"What'd you do that for?" I ask.

"You shoot the same things *all the time*," Max complains as I set my Avengers box and camera on the table. "We're not that interesting."

Nev rolls her eyes. "Max is cranky today," she explains, as if it wasn't totally obvious.

"Why?"

Max glares at us both. "Geometry test," he says, after another bite of sandwich.

"Wait!" I can't believe what I'm seeing. "Is that *salami*?"

Max ducks his head, acting shy.

"I have to get this on camera!" I pop the lens cap off, connect my external mic, and hit RECORD. Across from me, Nev cracks up.

NARRATOR
(documentary film voice)
Can you tell us why this is such a monumental occasion?

MAX
(scowls)

NEV pops into the frame.

NEV
For the past two years—

MAX
(correcting her)
No. Approximately two hundred sixty-eight school days.

I slip out of my chair to fit them both in the frame.

NEV
(continuing)
For the past two years, Max has brought the *same
sandwich*—ham and cheese on wheat with mus-
tard on one slice, mayo on the other—for lunch.
Every day.

(leaning back, triumphant)

It's weird. And now, something different.

CLOSE-UP: Max.

NEV
Why now? Why today?

CLOSE-UP: MAX's eyes dart from side to side and
a small muscle in his throat twitches.

I don't pull the camera away. This is a *moment.*

MAX swallows, then speaks directly into the
camera.

MAX
My dad made a salami sandwich for lunch on
Saturday. It smelled really good, and I couldn't stop

thinking about it. That was how I knew I had to switch.

He stops speaking, but I leave the camera on, held tight on his face. David Stonestreet, one of my favorite directors, said that people reveal more once they think they're done, when they stop paying attention to being filmed.

MAX's eyes get a little far away, like he can see the memory.

MAX

I was ready.

YES! There it is!

End scene.

The warning bell rings. I haven't even opened my mom-delivered lunch.

"Hey, when are we going to work on *The Spy Who Bugged Me?*" Nev asks. "We don't have a lot of time."

Max opens my lunchbox, fishes through it, and grabs an apple. "An apple a day blows the blues away!" He grins at an imaginary camera and takes a huge bite. Nev and I don't even bother to respond to that one.

"This weekend?" I offer. "We can do some shots outside of school, and maybe make the chase scene outside." We get up from the table and head for the doors.

"We have Spanish this weekend," Max says. "Don't you remember?"

"Totally," I lie.

Nev sees right through me.

"The skit," she says, giving me a nudge. "We're recording the skit."

"Totally," I repeat. Max waves as he goes toward social studies.

"Thanks for the apple!" he calls.

Shooting a Spanish skit. Shooting a spy movie. Shooting an extra credit video.

Three video projects at once? I got this.

THURSDAY NIGHT

All good directors learn as much as possible about their source material when they start a movie.

I'm determined to do that, too. I sit down with Jack's *A Sea of Serpents*, the laptop we share, and my language arts and Spanish folders. Research time!

Language arts extra credit first. Inside the back cover of the book, I find MK Nightshade's website address and type it in.

There's a link to audio from *A Sea of Serpents*—the soundtrack?—I click PLAY.

Haunting music comes out of the computer's speakers. It's a theme I recognize from the movie. I let it go while I poke around the site.

"The forest floor was thick with evergreen needles, and the mist deadened all sound."

I nearly jump out of my skin at the raspy whisper that suddenly fills my room. The voice goes on, and before I scream for my parents, I realize that it's reading *A Sea of Serpents*. The link must've been to an audio clip of the book.

I laugh at myself. I let the voice continue. It's kind of cool, hearing it.

I check out the site: There's a fan section with original art based on the books, a family tree to sort out the characters' relationships, which I don't really read—Thing is following the girl and his hot breath is just inches from her sleeping form, according to the book reader guy—but what stands out is that there's an interview with David Stonestreet—the guy who directed *Archangel's Revenge*, *Mountains of the Golden Sun*, and *Curse of the Janus Rocket*—only three of the best action movies I've seen in the past few years. Plus he's directing the next movie in this series, *A Mausoleum of Monsters*.

I click on it, and when I see how long it is, I download it to read later.

This is the best homework ever.

"Thing crept, unseen, unheard, yet always in the girl's shadow."

Back to the page. Underneath the director info—oooh! Production stills from *Mausoleum*, a link to an actor's blog about what it was like to be on the set, and character sketches for the sequels.

I read the blog entry and page through the production stills for *A Mausoleum of Monsters*, which releases in a couple of weeks. The shots are mainly of the cast in costume. Awesome.

I read the bio of the costume designer.

I click on the link to other films she's worked on, then go back to Nightshade's website. The book reader guy finishes the chapter. A pop-up covers my screen. *Download* A Sea of Serpents *audio! On sale NOW!* scrolls across it.

I kind of like hearing it. It reminds me of when my parents

used to read to me before bed. I click the link and go to the audio-book page. Just as I'm about to set up an account, my door opens with a bang.

"Time's up, squid. Log off." Jack plops on my bed, sweaty from track practice.

"Get off my bed! You stink!"

I'm sifting through my desk junk drawer for a gift card that I can use to buy the $12.99 book. Something soft whumps the back of my head.

"Log *off*!" Yesterday's dirty socks splat on the floor.

"Wait your turn," I snap, not taking my eyes away from the screen. "I got on at seven thirty." We each get the laptop for an hour.

Jack's bony finger taps the upper right corner of the screen: 8:32. He knocks on my head, too.

What?! Is there a mistake on the computer? Did he mess with it? I spin around—my clock and phone all read the same time.

I've lost my hour.

Jack leans over me—reeking armpit in my face, so I squeal and elbow him in the ribs—and logs me off.

"Should pay more attention, squid," he says. I can't get the computer back until after he's done. I lost my audiobook link, and probably the sale price. Not to mention that I'm supposed to be getting this video ready and I hadn't found anything I could use yet. And I haven't gotten the Spanish shooting script together. So much for being on top of things.

Hopelessness rises through me, and I put my forehead on the

desk. If I don't get my language arts grade up, I don't show my movie in the Hoot. I'll let my friends down.

I could fight the bad thoughts, like Mr. Sinclair suggests, but why bother? They wash over me in waves.

Failing feels awful.

FRIDAY NIGHT

"Mouse Trap! Or Apples to Apples?" Mom's muffled voice comes from the closet in the den. It's Friday Night Fun. Once a month, the four of us stay home, eat popcorn, play board games, and watch movies. Mom got the idea from a parenting magazine, and our family's been doing it since before I got here. Mom's kind of obsessed. An asteroid could be on a collision course with Earth and she'd insist we finish our turns in Monopoly.

Tonight, I'm grateful for the distraction and glad no one's talking to me about school.

Jack's got the opposite problem. He's standing in the middle of the family room, arms crossed and scowling.

"C'mon, Mom! Charlie's mom said she'd drive both ways, so you don't even have to leave." He wants to go see *War Troopers of Blendon*, which opens tonight. I don't know why he wants to go—from the online trailer, I can tell that the story is predictable and the effects aren't anything special. But Jack likes to watch stuff explode, so . . .

I take out my camera and turn it on. This might get good.

MOM

(still in closet)

Mouse Trap! Or Apples to Apples?

JACK

You aren't listening to me!

MOM

I am listening; I'm just choosing not to respond.
Mouse Trap! Or Apples to Apples? We haven't
played either in ages. It's your turn to pick, Jack.

JACK

Neither! I'm not playing.

JACK storms out of the room. Camera follows his
back through the kitchen to the foot of the stairs.
Before climbing, he spins quickly, reaches out, and
grabs the lens.

Darkness.

He pulls the camera out of my hands.

"Hey!"

"Knock. It. Off," he says through gritted teeth. He thrusts the
camera into my chest and takes the stairs two at a time. His door
slams before I move again.

Mom pokes her head around the doorframe.

"We're starting in ten minutes. I chose Apples to Apples," she tells me, the bright red box tucked under one arm and a fake smile stuck to her face.

I point upstairs. "Jack's not going to play."

"Too bad." She shrugs, like it doesn't matter to her, but her eyes give her away: They're dark and hurt-looking. My heart hurts for her. She looks forward to Friday Night Fun, and it's not fair of Jack to wreck it.

"Where's Dad?"

"Puttering in the office, trying to work," she explains. "He'll be out in a few minutes." Together, we clear the papers, junk mail, school notices, and decorative bowl off the dining room table. It's the only space in the house where my super-organized mom loses the Clutter Creep Battle, as she calls it. In the kitchen, I get the red-and-white popcorn bowl from the cabinet and she pulls out the old-school air popper.

She plugs it in and it whines like a hair dryer. I hand her the jar of popcorn and hop up to sit on the counter. She frowns at me but doesn't say anything, so I stay while Mom buzzes around the kitchen, getting the tray for the bowls, drinks, and dish of mixed nuts that Dad munches on.

The first kernels pop in small, short explosions. *PA-CHEW! PA-CHING! PA-PA-PA-PA!* I slide the bowl under the spout to catch the white, fluffy results. Their smell is a comfort. It reminds me of when I was a few years younger, before I found out about my disorder, when I was just a "quirky kid," according to Dad, not one that had a problem that needed to be "managed." Suddenly, a feeling hits me so strong I have to hang on to the edge of the counter because I'm afraid it's going to make me tip over. It's not sadness, exactly, it's more . . . wishful. I struggle to name it, and then it comes to me: It's longing. A longing for things to be the way they were when I was eight or nine: one or two homework sheets a night, no projects, and not disappointing everyone all the time.

The bowl fills quickly, the smell fills the kitchen, and then all that's left are a few scorched kernels, clacking in the empty chamber. I know how they feel. Mom unplugs the machine.

I grab a handful of hot, dry, snacky goodness. If I just keep sitting here and thinking, I might cry.

"Can't even wait for the butter, huh?" Mom asks.

I shrug.

Dad comes into the kitchen.

"How'd it go?" Mom asks. He tightens his lips into a frown. Not good, I guess.

"Hey, muffin." He grabs a handful of popcorn, too, and kisses my head. "Where's Jack?"

"Upstairs. Teenager-ing." Mom brushes her hand back and forth, like she's wiping Jack off the table. "We'll play without him."

Dad looks like he wants to ask more questions, but stops himself. "Okay."

The three of us sit around the table in our regular seats and Mom opens the Apples to Apples box. I can't remember the last time we had Friday Night Fun with just us—had we ever? Maybe when Jack was sick with mono last year? I try to shake this weird feeling.

Mom deals the cards and we play. Dad sets up a barricade so that no one can see his cards. It's a quieter game than usual; Jack always makes the funniest analogies.

"*Awkward*," Dad reads. I throw in *oil spill*. Mom goes for *Kardashians*. Mom wins.

"Good one, Hess," Dad offers.

"*Lovely*," Mom reads from a card. Should I go with *silence* or *redwood forest*? I drop *silence*. Dad chooses *roses*. Mom laughs. I win.

After a few more rounds, the snacks get low and Mom leaves to fire up the popper again. I have that sensation like someone is looking at me. I glance up, just in time to see Jack's head pull back around the doorframe. He's spying.

"All are welcome," I say loudly. Dad snaps his head in my direction. It's a line from *Poltergeist*. I tilt my chin toward the door. Jack hovers there, an unhappy ghost.

"Where's Mom?"

In the kitchen, the popper whines.

He slides into the room and perches on the edge of his seat, ready to disappear if someone says the wrong thing. He must've showered while up there—his hair is wet and he smells soapy.

"Want in?" Dad points to the cards.

Indecision flits across his face. He wants to play, but part of him—a big part—is still mad that he's missing the movie with his friends. He doesn't say anything. Dad hands him cards.

"Just in case," he says.

The popcorn explosions start. Jack seems ready to bolt. I shift in my seat.

"Don't bring out your camera," he growls at me.

"I don't even have it!" It's not allowed at FNF. Which sucks.

"You shouldn't be allowed to record people in the house," he goes on. His anger comes at me, white-hot. "This isn't a reality show. It's my life."

"I didn't *do* anything!" I drop my cards and push away from the table.

"You did! You totally got in my face," he goes on.

"Hey!" Dad speaks sharply, over our rising argument and the top of his card protection wall. "This is not the time or place. Jack, Hess doesn't have a camera. Hess, don't film your brother. End of story."

My brother and I glare at each other across the table. His cheeks splotch red and his jaw is tight. I give him my best narrow eyes of doom.

Mom returns with the popcorn.

"You in?" she asks Jack.

He nods, not saying anything.

We pick up with a new round, the words and feelings as fragile as glass.

After a few hands, Dad reads, "*Dramatic.*" Jack throws down *teenager*.

Mom laughs. The tension in the room drains—not completely, but just enough.

And that's enough for now.

‹‹ FAST-FORWARD ››

- Watch *Super 8* on the couch with Mom
- Stay up really late getting the Spanish stuff ready
- Don't finish; get up early

‹‹ RESUME PLAY ››

SATURDAY AFTERNOON

"Hey, señora," I say as Nev comes into my room. She perches the giant sombrero from Jack's birthday at Arriba's on her head and wraps my blue throw blanket around her like a poncho.

"It's señorita," Max says.

Nev rattles off some Spanish that I probably should be able to understand by now but don't. I'm really good at asking for a glass of water, though.

Nev flops on my bed, big hat hiding not only her face but most of her chest.

"Now I can see why there are so many pictures of people asleep in one of these things," she says. "Sombreros are *comfy*!"

"That's a stereotype," I mumble. "And we're not using those. We're using cowboy costumes. It's a Western." I adjust the camera on the tripod, which is pointed at the backdrop that Max is still painting. We are going all out for this assignment. I fight off a yawn. It's been a long day already and we haven't even started shooting.

"Ándale, Max!" Nev says. "I need to be home by six."

"It's four thirty," Max says. "Chill out, amiga." He puts the paintbrush down and turns toward us. "Oh! Hey! How's this: Chill out with Billy's Frozen Flan! So creamy, it's dreamy!"

"Terrible," Nev mutters. I giggle.

Max sighs and adds the finishing touches on his cactus and ranch house, and I pass out the scripts we wrote—okay, Nev and Max did most of the Spanish lines; I did the shot list.

"Did you rewrite it?" Max says, fanning the pages. "It's, like, a two-minute skit, not a thirty-minute TV show."

"It's a shooting script," I explain. "It has more than just your dialogue in it. It lists all the shots I need. Without it, I'd have no plan."

Nev snorts. "You, plan something? That's hilarious."

"Really, Nev?" I say. I stick my tongue out at her.

"Well, you *don't*," she responds.

Do I want to go down this road? We don't have a lot of time. I take a breath, hold it for the count of five. Let it out.

"There's a first time for everything," I say, hoping it's enough to end things.

Nev doesn't answer. Instead, she pushes the costumes to the side and she and Max look at their scripts.

Spanish Skit: Where Is the Horse?

EXT. The desert.

MARIA sits in front of a cactus. The sun beats down. It's hot. PACO enters from offscreen.

PACO
Where did the horse go?

MARIA

(looks around)

The horse?

PACO

Yes, the horse! My horse!

CLOSE-UP: MARIA.

MARIA

(shrugs)

I don't know. Where did you leave the horse?

WIDE SHOT: PACO.

PACO

(pointing to cactus)

Right there! You were watching it!

MARIA

I'm sorry. The horse left.

PACO

(getting angry)

Where did it go?

MARIA

(testily)

I don't know.

PACO stomps to the far side of the set and whistles.

PACO

Hombre! Come!

Hoofbeats from off camera. HOMBRE appears,
dusty from being in the desert.

HOMBRE

(whinnies)

PACO

You returned!

MARIA

There is the horse!

End scene.

"I thought you were going to be in it?" Max asks from his spot
on the floor. "We had lines for you."

"I *am* in it. I'm doing the camera stuff. I kept the lines, just gave
them back to you guys." I adjust the tripod and zoom in so you
can't see the walls of my room. The backdrop fills the screen.

"We're all supposed to have a part," Nev points out, sitting up.

"I do have a part," I say. My face heats and my gut bubbles. "I'm also Hombre." I point to the stuffed brown pony on my bed. He's dusty from the basement, which is great—instant authenticity.

"Señora Garciaparra is not going to give us credit if we don't all participate."

"Let it go, Nev. I helped write the script. I'm shooting the skit. I am the horse. What else is there?" My voice is a little louder than it probably should be.

"Um, speak Spanish?" Max says quietly. "That's kind of the point of this—to speak Spanish."

I'm not good at speaking Spanish. I don't want to be in front of the camera. I'm tired and want to capture this before they have to go home.

"You can't record your way out of this," Nev says.

Heat flashes through my body. What is her deal? For as long as we've been friends, Nev's known that I don't like doing stuff in front of people. I try to control myself and think of a way out of the situation.

"Look," I say, making a peace offering, "how about I record a voice-over at the beginning, introducing our skit and who we are? In Spanish," I add, in case they don't get it.

Nev and Max have a silent conversation with raised eyebrows, cocked heads, and shrugs.

"Fine," Nev says. "At least that way, if Señora doesn't give all of us credit because you didn't participate enough, we can argue that you did something."

"We're going to get credit," I say, brushing off her comment. "But we won't get anything if we don't do it."

"Let's get started," Max says.

"Places!" I say. I hold up my clapper board, a souvenir that my uncle brought back from a visit to Epic Studios. "*Where Is the Horse?* Scene one. And . . . action!"

I scramble behind the camera and hit RECORD. Max takes his place in front of the cactus. He reads the lines from his script, stumbling through the Spanish. Nev responds, the words rolling off her tongue like she's a native speaker, not like she spent her childhood watching *Dora the Explorer*, but trips over the hem of her huge cowboy jacket.

We do it again, but Max flubs a line.

And has a sneezing fit during take three.

"Max!" Nev snaps. She fans herself with the prop ten-gallon hat.

"El caballo es demasiado . . . *polvoriento!*" he says.

"Reset." I point them to their places. "This time, Max, make sure you hit your mark so you don't block Nev." He rolls his eyes and makes funny faces through take four.

Nev loses her place during take five. She takes off the jacket and there's a damp spot on her back. "These things are *hot*," she grumbles.

"Cut!" I holler, midway through take six. "Cut!"

"What?" Max says.

"You could totally tell that you were reading the script," I tell them. "It was obvious."

"But we *were* reading it," Nev says.

"It didn't look good."

"It was three words," Max throws in.

"It's been six takes. Don't you have it memorized by now? I do."

Silence. That sounded *way* snarky, but still . . . it's not like the script is long! It's barely a page.

They stare at me: Nev, wearing her DIY costume and the silly hat, her eyes slowly narrowing, and Max, mouth open, like he can't believe what he's seeing. Shame threatens to take over, but I push it down and ignore it. This needs to look good.

Nev moves first. Slowly puts the hat on the floor. Then she peels off the jacket and drops it from the tips of her fingers, like it's infested with something nasty. Her hairline is damp.

"We're done here," she says. Without another word, she pushes past me, grabs her backpack off the floor, and leaves. Deep down, I know she's right. It was a jerky move. Max is still frozen.

"Um, yeah. Well, that was not cool, Hess," he says finally. "Not cool."

Like Nev, he walks off the set and grabs his backpack.

"You know," he tosses over his shoulder, "this could've been fun . . . but it's not a game."

He butchered the quote, but I got the point.

‹‹ FAST-FORWARD ››

- Moping for the rest of Saturday
- Cleaning the garage while Dad supervises
- Shooting exteriors in the park down the street

‹‹ RESUME PLAY ››

THREE WEEKS AGO

SUNDAY NIGHT

After my mess of a weekend, on Sunday night I'm sitting at the laptop, listening to *A Sea of Serpents*, trying to forget that my friends hate me. Jack's out seeing *War Troopers of Blendon* finally, which means I get to keep the computer.

I've downloaded the takes from the Spanish skit and edited them into a great short. I even went through other footage I shot this weekend, and saved what I want to keep for our spy movie to my external hard drive. Unlike the folders Mom set up for my assignments, the way I organize my camera footage makes sense: *Crowd Shots, School-Interior, School-Exterior, Home-Interior, Home-Exterior*, and so on.

I've poked around on some movie review sites (just like I thought, all of my favorite reviewers trashed *War Troopers*) but nothing holds my attention for too long. I try to read the interview with the *Mausoleum of Monsters* director, but I keep getting distracted. It reminds me of language arts, and that reminds me of how bad everything is lately—my grades, my friends . . . fighting with Jack. It's exhausting. I need to put something right. I rub my eyes and stretch, just as Sir Oakheart slays Thing and saves the girl. I wait for the scene to end, listening to every word.

My language arts folder is on top of the pile of papers on my floor. Ms. "I believe in tests, not extra credit" Walker is letting me make a movie. I'd be stupid not to get started.

I open a blank document in my scriptwriting software and stare at the screen. I need a concept—an idea—to get my project going. What can I say to MK Nightshade in a two-minute movie? What can I show that will get me as many points as possible? I lean back in my chair and close my eyes, letting the words in the audiobook carry me away.

No book has ever carried me anywhere, before now. Huh.

Thing's blood dripped from the sword onto the leaves. In the weak moonlight, it pattered down, a black rain. Sir Oakheart motioned to the girl. "Come." She shook her head: No.

That's not in the film!

I up the volume, heart pounding. The girl doesn't go to Sir Oakheart, and instead acts upset with him for killing Thing. She won't speak to him. Whoa. And then . . .

"You are an uncommon hero, who murders without permission," she snapped.

There's my angle.

I toggle back to the blank script and pause the book so I don't miss anything good.

I type: Sir Oakheart: An Uncommon Hero.

Sir Oakheart: An Uncommon Hero

EXT. Day. Close-up of pirate ship, on high seas.

NARRATOR

An epic journey for an epic hero . . .

EXT. Ship tossed in a storm, sea serpent attacks the boat.

(Note: Serpent is a bathtub toy.)

NARRATOR

. . . but one who is not who he seems.

FAST MONTAGE: Famous faces, funny faces, cartoon faces.

NARRATOR

Sir Oakheart swore to uphold the law of the land, protect the innocent, and above all, to never break the Knight's Code.

So why would he?

MUSIC: "Who Do You See in the Mirror," by Theo Christmas.

INT. A castle great room. SIR OAKHEART practicing his swordplay.

CUT TO: A close-up of hands on the hilt.

NARRATOR

Creatures live and die by your hands,
Sir Oakheart.

CUT TO: SEA SERPENT close-up.

NARRTOR

And you never answer to anyone.

FAST MONTAGE: Faces, repeated, only more quickly.

NARRATOR

At all.

Beat.

This time, you have to.

IMAGE: GIRL, cradling THING's dead body.

CUT TO:

EXT. The deck of a ship. SIR OAKHEART raises his sword to the sky.

MONDAY

Monday morning, I spot Nev and Max in the main hall and before they can be huffy with me I give them my biggest puppy dog eyes.

"I was a jerk. On Saturday. A prima donna. I'm really sorry." My expression might be silly, but my words are sincere. "I edited what we shot and it looks really good." I bat my eyelashes and wave a memory stick. "Wanna see it?"

"Your eyes look like some freaky doll's. Stop doing that," Nev says. She's juggling her duffel bag of clothes and her backpack. She lugs everything back and forth between her dad's and mom's because she says it reminds them that the divorce may have made their lives better, but it made hers harder.

Nev doesn't mess around.

I keep dodging in front of her, so she can't look away. She's scowling, but there's a hint of a smile under her grumpy face. I just have to make her laugh.

I make my eyes even bigger. They ache from being stretched.

"Forgive *meeee*?" I whine. Max cracks first.

"Dork," he says, and grins. Nev follows.

"¿Está bien?" she says. "Let's watch it during lunch."

The first bell rings. I jet to my locker and rummage through it for my books. Knowing that Nev, Max, and I are okay—and that

I have a script for my extra credit project—makes me feel like nothing can take me down. Not even the slightly greenish-tinged orange that I spot under a copy of an old science lab report. I cover it back up, close the door, and head to homeroom.

I even beat the late bell.

☆　　☆　　☆

I spend most of language arts working on my extra credit project while Ms. Walker goes on and on about fitting into society—a theme in the book I'm supposed to be reading for class but haven't yet.

"The life where nothing was ever unexpected. Or inconvenient. Or unusual. The life without color, pain, or past," Ms. Walker reads. She closes the book. "This is what their society wants. Nothing messy or difficult. Only Sameness," she says.

I *so* wouldn't fit into that society.

I draw eight boxes on a sheet of notebook paper, and I sketch a scene in each one. Underneath the bottom of each box, I jot a one-sentence summary of the shot.

I don't look out the window once.

After a while, I stop hearing Ms. Walker's voice. All I see are the mini-scenes in front of me, connecting and growing into a movie.

"Hess? . . . Hess . . . *Hester*!"

Snapping back to reality, I am sitting in an empty classroom. Or nearly empty. Ms. Walker stands in front of my desk, hands on her hips. Her glasses have slid down her nose, giving her a totally typical grouchy-teacher look.

"Uhh," I say. I sink lower in my seat.

"You missed the bell. And the late bell," Ms. Walker says.

"I have lunch now," I say stupidly.

"The only reason why I let you sit here is because I've never seen you so focused. What on earth are you doing?"

I hug my notebook to my chest. Both the notebook and I are equally flat.

"Uhhh, working on my extra credit project." My ears burn.

Ms. Walker's face scrunches, like she's trying not to laugh — or yell. She takes a deep breath and blows it out of her mouth. She puts both hands on my desk; leans over. Her sandy hair slips out from behind her ears.

"While I'm very, very glad that you are preparing to do the extra credit assignment, Hester, your priority needs to be what is going on in this classroom." She speaks super slowly, like she's not sure I'd understand otherwise. "You need to get your grades up. Your *test* grades. Extra credit isn't enough. You will fail unless you pass these tests. Got it?"

I gulp, then nod. But I'm pretty sure that I'm never going to get my test grades up to where she wants them.

"Have you even read the book we're discussing?"

I squirm in my seat. "I saw the movie," I admit, wishing my life were a movie and I could cut the scene right now.

She winces. "I just . . ." She stops, breathes. Straightens. "Go to lunch, Hess."

I scramble out of my chair and stuff my notebook in my bag. Bolt.

Cut.

MONDAY LUNCH

"¿Dónde está el caballo?" Max says in a high-pitched voice, cracking himself—and us—up. We're huddled around one of the library computers, watching the edited version of our Spanish skit that's due this afternoon.

"So you like it?" I ask for the third—okay, maybe fifth—time.

"It's great," Max says. He pulls a granola bar from his pocket and holds it up for us to see. "Crunchy, munchy, yummy! Try FigFabulous granola bars!"

Nev and I roll our eyes.

"The movie came out great," Nev says. She warmed up when the outtakes came on after the skit ended, and was actually laughing out loud by the time it was done.

I'd spliced together the best of the six takes to make the actual skit, and recorded the voice-over. Once that was done, I decided that since I had so much extra footage, I may as well use it. I put together a blooper reel with Nev tripping, Max sneezing, and me knocking over the set (which I shot after they left)—only speeded up and repeated.

"I wish we thought to make a commercial," Max said. "That would have been great."

Nev laughs. "Not if you wrote it!"

"Hey!" Max says, but he knows Nev is kidding.

"Next time," I say. We watch it one more time.

"We are creating Spanish *fusion*!" Max says.

"Huh?" Nev and I look at each other.

"From *School of Rock*?" he shrugs. "Musical fusion? Spanish fusion?" He is so bad with movie quotes.

I groan. "You are hopeless."

"But our skit is *killer*," Max says.

We high-five. "Those thirty points are ours," he finishes.

While he and Nev watch it again, I lean back in my seat, relieved. Thirty points should keep my grade at a low C. Passing.

"What about *The Spy Who Bugged Me*?" Nev asks as I eject the drive and we say good-bye to the librarian. The bell buzzes.

"We're behind," I say. "We need to shoot more this week in order for it to be ready for the Hoot."

"Then let's do it," says Max. We plan to meet up after school later in the week and head to class.

I stop at my locker.

"Why don't you come over this weekend and we can plan out the rest of the shoot?" Nev asks as I grab our science workbook, causing a landslide.

A banana—a really old one—rides the wave of junk. In a second, I'm marooned in a pile of paper topped with gnarly fruit, which I'm pretty sure has splooshed against my shin. Laughter bounces around the hall.

"The Hoot is only two weeks away, and they want forms in by

Monday," Nev says. She leans against the bank of lockers as I bend to scoop up the mess.

"Sure," I say, "No problem."

There's a boogery-looking banana smear on my jeans, and the rest of the banana has oozed all over my math homework . . . from January. *That's* where that was!

I slide the top layer of goo-covered stuff into the oversized hall garbage can and origami the rest into the locker, finally slamming the door.

"Your mom would poop purple Twinkies if she saw that," Nev says as we speed walk to beat the bell.

"That's pretty much what Mr. Sinclair does on his inspections," I respond. He checks my locker twice a month. "Last time he looked the banana was probably fresh. It's probably good that he didn't see how bad it got."

Nev glances at the smear on my leg. "Yeah. Be glad."

I nudge her with my elbow. "You got a problem with it, Chatterjee?"

She throws a wicked grin. "With what? Your aroma?" Only she draws it out like *ah-roh-maah*. "Oh, yeah, I got problems with it. You smell like an old dessert."

"Like a rose, you mean."

"Like moldy banana bread," she says.

We slide into our chairs just as the bell rings. Usually I feel as off-kilter as the inside of my locker. But today they liked the Spanish skit.

Today is a success.

TUESDAY AFTERNOON

There's a pirate ship in my basement, I'm sure of it. Jack and I played with it when we were little. Surrounded by boxes, with dust floating everywhere, I sneeze six times in a row. My eyes water.

The upstairs door creaks open and heavy feet thunk on the stairs.

"Gesundheit?" my dad says. "Were those sneezes or cannon fire?"

"Very funny." I sniff, then sneeze again.

He thunks the rest of the way down and picks his way across the trail of wreckage I've left across the concrete floor. Stooping, he comes up with a glittery wreath that Mom hangs around the holidays dangling from his good arm.

"Probably shouldn't leave that there?" I offer. He nods and awkwardly places it on a shelf.

"What's the damage for?"

"A project," I say, eyes back on the boxes lining the shelves across our longest basement wall. I've checked in every black Sharpied one marked *Toys* or *Jack + Hess* in Mom's neat printing.

"Need help?" Dad sneezes as I slide another box (*Blocks*) off the shelf. "We really should clean this stuff out," he adds.

"Sure," I say, responding to his question. He steps closer and we pull the flaps back. The box is filled with—duh—wooden blocks. "I need a pirate ship."

I move the boxes, Dad helps me open them. We find a mini-bake oven that never quite cooked stuff all the way through, Jack's Hot Wheels collection, and some old games and puzzles. No ship. Maybe Mom got rid of it?

"Success!" Dad says, pulling the ship out of *Water/bath toys* with one arm. Both of us sneeze as a cloud of dust follows it out of the box. Dad hands it over, and I do a quick inspection: Sails seem a little tattered, but otherwise it's okay. I tuck it under my arm, head for the stairs.

"Ummm, Hess?" Dad calls. I stop. "Forgetting something?" He gestures at the boxes, bags, and loose toys all over the floor.

I groan.

"Dad! I promise I'll clean it up later. I just really want to get started on this project . . ." He slowly shakes his head, a tiny smile on his face.

I run the ship aground on the steps and face him. "Help me out?" I ask hopefully.

He gestures with his sling. "Oh, sure."

He supervises while I get the basement put back together to Mom's satisfaction.

"Grog and hardtack?" he asks, once the last box is put back where it belongs.

"Aye aye, Captain!" I answer, and we head upstairs.

« PAUSE »

Mom's got a lot to say about Dad and me. For instance: We're "cut from the same cloth."

I get what she means. Mom's the "getter-doner" in the house: organizing stuff, planning things, keeping us all in order. Dad is . . . *flaky* isn't the right word . . . he's kind of *preoccupied*, I guess. He's a freelance writer, doing articles for magazines, newspapers, and other clients. So he kind of works from home. He's either holed up in his office on a deadline, or out interviewing someone, or doing a million things at the same time and not quite getting through all of them. Also, he gets so into his work that he forgets to do stuff.

Like picking me up from school.

By the time I was in third grade I was used to it, but as a kindergartener it freaked me out. Jack, who was in fourth grade, tried to calm me down as I cried the first time in the principal's office.

"You'll get used to it, Hessie," he said, handing me tissue after tissue. "Dad doesn't mean it."

And when Dad showed up, apologizing like crazy, face gray-white and eyes as big as teacups, I saw that Jack was right.

Now that I walk to school and know how to make a few basic meals, it's much easier. When Mom got Dad a smartphone, things really changed. He sets alarms for stuff, Mom manages their shared calendar, and he hasn't forgotten us in a while.

« RESUME PLAY »

TUESDAY
AFTERNOON — KITCHEN

"What're you working on?" I ask him once we get upstairs. I grab the roll of paper towels and some cleaner to dust off the ship.

Dad gets the bag of Vienna Fingers cookies, hands two to each of us, leans against the cabinets, and runs his good hand through his hair, making it stick up.

"A *Weekender* article on the new bakery that's in town. The family just immigrated to America and they are really making a go of their dream." He chews and talks and I eat and spritz.

"I need to go and interview them this weekend, and I'm wondering if it'd be okay if I borrowed your camera."

"Sure," I say.

Then I tune in, for real. I stop cleaning the ship and turn to him.

"You want to borrow my *camera*?"

"Yeah," he says. "My digital voice recorder is good for an interview, but I can't take notes about the setting and the ambience the way I usually do. I thought if I shot footage with your camera, I could just play it back when I was writing and get all the details I need." He looks pleased with himself for coming up with that solution.

I frown. Dad doesn't have a steady hand with the camera in general, and if he's trying to talk to someone *and* shoot, he's going to get a lot of ceiling and floor shots. And ones that make him queasy. I sigh.

"Why don't I just come with you and shoot? That way you can concentrate on the interview part. I can even set up a tripod or something and record the interview, so that way you won't have to worry about taking notes at all. You just have to get their permission first."

A wide smile splits his face. "Thanks, honey. That would be great. I'll give them a call." He disappears to his office, and I go back to my pirate ship.

It's only later that I realize that he had no intention of borrowing my camera at all—he knew I'd never go for it. I shake my head at how easily I was played.

LATER TUESDAY

The pirate ship bobs in the tub, a newly purchased LEGO Sir Oakheart stuck to the deck. I attached him with some double-sided tape, but every time it gets wet, he tips.

My back aches from leaning over, but I can't get the shot right unless the camera is on the same wall as the faucet. And I need to get the shot right, because I'm running out of time. It's due Thursday. I stretch and try again.

With my left hand, I swish the water into waves. Getting the color right required mixing the rest of the Blueberry Blast Hyper Hues hair dye Jack uses for track meets and one of my mom's fizzy bath balls. The boat rides the waves; Sir Oakheart holds steady.

I give the water one more swish, then grab the camera.

[RECORD]

CLOSE-UP: Deck.

CLOSE-UP: SIR OAKHEART.

CLOSE-UP: Waves.

CLOSE-UP: Waves against the side of the boat.

I stir the sea again, then slip my old dragon puppet—doubling as a sea serpent—over my right hand. I sink my elbow into the ocean. The hem of the puppet gets wet.

CLOSE-UP: Waves crashing over the boat's deck.
CLOSE-UP: SERPENT's head.

WIDE SHOT: Boat on the sea.

I'm breathing through my mouth, even though I've muted the audio. Body noises are a pain to edit out, so I'll just add ocean sounds in later.

The overhead light is too bright, but the software will darken everything. I put the camera on the floor, swirl the sea, pick up the camera, make the puppet menace the ship.

PAN: Whole ship.

There's a rapid knocking on the bathroom door.
"Hess! Hester! Are you okay?"
I nearly drop my camera.

[PAUSE]

"Mom! What are you doing?! I'm fine!" I call. I thought I'd be done before she got home from work.

"I've been calling your name for ten minutes. Are you sick in there? Did something . . . happen?"

"No! Oh, no! Just doing some shooting!"

"Can you open the door so we don't have to talk like this?"

"Umm . . ." I don't really want to, because when she sees the tub, she's going to flip the heck out.

"Open the door, Hess." It's her no-nonsense voice.

I straighten from my crouched position next to the tub, and a silver line of pain zings across my back. I wince, and catch my reflection in the mirror: The extra-bright lights make the dark circles under my eyes stand out. My braces glitter.

She's frowning when the door opens. "Dinnertime," she says. There's a deep crease across her forehead.

Had I really been working that long? I catch a whiff of garlicky spaghetti sauce coming from downstairs. Guess so.

But standing there, taking that whiff, was one whiff too long. Mom's eyes widen like a character in a horror movie's, right before they get a cleaver to the noggin.

"Your hands!"

I glance down. My left hand, the one that's been swirling the tub-ocean, is a dead-body shade of blue. And rivers of the same color run down my right arm from the elbow.

"It's just hair dye and stuff," I say quickly. "No big deal."

Her glance bounces over my head. "The *tub*!"

"I'll clean it."

She squeezes past me. "Yeah, you will," she says. "It's so . . ." She can't even finish, just stands there, shaking her head.

With every swish and swirl, each time I created a wave, the

water left marks higher and higher along the white sides of the tub: dark blue marks.

Oops.

"Dinner. Now. Then . . ." She reaches under the sink and puts the yellow cleaning supplies basket on the counter. "This."

I pull the plug on Sir Oakheart and leave him—and my extra credit—marooned.

REALLY LATE TUESDAY

My right elbow is blue. So are the cuticles on my left hand.

After almost an hour of scrubbing, the tub is now the color of the light blue hydrangeas in our front yard. Although it's an improvement from when I started, Mom is not psyched.

The Hyper Hues package reads, "Will stain most surfaces." They aren't lying. I should've paid attention before I poured it into the tub.

I lean back in my chair and rub my eyes. It's 11:35 p.m. Jack finally surrendered the laptop, and I've been editing for two hours.

I need to add the credits and title sequence, and tighten up the soundtrack transitions with the cuts. Ms. Walker will totally give me a bunch of extra credit points for it. Hopefully enough to help me pass.

A yawn nearly splits my face in half. I have to get some sleep. I should also probably read some stuff for social studies and do some math. But before I do, I want to check out the screen stills from *Sea of Serpents* that I'd copied for reference.

I close the video software and open a browser. A few googles later, and not only do I have the still images, but alternate shots and the shooting script and a headache.

And the next time I look at the clock, it's close to one a.m.

Eyes gritty and back still aching from cleaning the Bathtub Sea, I don't even bother doing any other homework, brushing my teeth, or putting on pajamas. I just crawl under my covers.

WEDNESDAY MORNING

I hit snooze three times, then I drag myself to my desk and watch the video. I tweak some transitions, mess with the tone on the narration (I used my best deep voice when I recorded it) until I have to pee so bad I might explode. I race into the hall and nearly collide with crazy bed-head Jack, who is heading in the same direction.

He throws an elbow, pitching me off-balance, but there's no way I'm going to let him beat me to the bathroom—he'll be in there forever, and I won't make it downstairs. I stomp on his foot, hard, and when he yowls, I race in.

"You are so dead," he yells through the door.

I flush and turn the water on in the sink extra hard, taking my time as I wash my hands. Jack yanks the door as I turn the knob, and he pushes past me to the toilet.

I leave the door wide open as I go back to my room.

"Close it!" he yells. So I do (slowly), and I giggle as he jumps from foot to foot, waiting for me to be out of sight.

WEDNESDAY

My concentration is worse when I'm tired, and I bump and shuffle through school like an extra in *Night of the Living Dead*. I don't even bring out my camera once.

Thankfully, Ms. Walker is out sick. The sub has a tattoo and ponytail and no hope of controlling us. She puts the TV on and shows a lame teen drama adaptation of *Romeo and Juliet* that I've seen too many times. At least I manage to catch a twenty-minute nap while they kiss.

If this were a movie, I'd wake up refreshed and ready to tackle anything. Or maybe I'd open my eyes and find everyone gone, victims of some crazy alien abduction. I'd be the last girl on the planet.

But this is not a movie. I come back to consciousness with drool on my sleeve and, as Sarah helpfully points out, a big crease across my cheek.

"You are a disaster," she mutters. The sub is camped out behind Ms. Walker's desk, pretending to look at some papers but obviously playing with her phone. Sarah and I could probably have a dance-off and she wouldn't care.

"Thanks for the info," I respond with as much sarcasm as I can. She turns back to the movie. "Romeo" is showing "Juliet" a sleeping pill. I rub my cheek, hoping the crease—and Sarah—will go away.

It wasn't always like this between us. In elementary school, Sarah and I were friends. Well, like in first and second grade we were. Then she became super perfect—answering all the questions, always neat and quiet—while I became more and more out of control and lost. It got harder for me to keep stuff straight, and that made her mad for some reason. By fourth grade, we'd gone in opposite directions. I found movies and Nev, and she did whatever she did. But we never went back to being friendly.

Just before the bell rings, the sub passes out a study guide for our next test. I groan and stuff it in my bag, not even bothering to put it in a folder. Or look at it.

The bell rings, and as everyone grabs their books and bags and stuff, the sub calls out, "Hester Greene! Wait!"

I stop at the desk while she shuffles through Ms. Walker's papers.

"Hester . . . that's a cool name," she says while she looks. "Family name?"

I adjust the strap of my messenger bag. "It's after a character in some book my mom really liked. *The Scarlet Letter*?"

"Cool. I'm supposed to remind you of something . . . where is it?"

I shift from foot to foot while she searches. I'm hungry and tired and I want to caffeinate myself at lunch so I can stay awake for the rest of the day.

"Here it is!" She pulls a printed-out email from the pile and reads it. "*Remind Hester Greene that her extra credit project is due tomorrow.*" She glances up at me. "Extra credit! You must do really well in this class!"

Oh, crud. Out of nowhere, I remember that we're going out to dinner tonight with my aunt and uncle. Dad and Uncle Joe will go on and on about the Red Sox and their jobs and we'll be at the restaurant until the next ice age. I won't have time to finish my edits. My movie is going to suck, and there goes my grade.

I mumble something and leave.

I wish everyone *had* been abducted by aliens.

LATER

« UPLOAD »

The little arrow on my screen hovers over the button, switching it from gray to red, red to gray.

Should I click?

I grabbed the laptop before Jack got home and blew through the last of the edits. Some of the transitions are sloppy, but I'm out of time. For at least ten minutes, Mom and Dad have been calling me to come downstairs so we can leave.

I could spend all night tweaking it, but I want to be done with language arts and MK Nightshade.

It's fine, I tell myself. *Let it go.* There's other stuff to work on.

Like the test. Like social studies. Like Spanish. And our Hoot movie.

I add a few tags so later I can categorize it on my private YouChannel account: #MKNightshade #extracredit.

It's good. It will give me the points I need.

It better.

I breathe in and out. Strategies At Work.

Fine.

Click.

The wheel spins, the progress bar lights up, and seconds later "Sir Oakheart: Uncommon Hero" is live on my YouChannel.

The privacy settings box appears, and I send the link to Ms. Walker. I should dump it on a memory stick, too.

"Hess! Come on!" my mom calls from downstairs. "We're going to be late!"

No time.

I push back from my desk and head out. Smell ya later, Ms. Walker.

‹‹ FAST-FORWARD ››

- Eat a ton of mussels so I don't have to talk much
- Dad goes on and on about the bakery interview
- Crawl into bed
- Head to school

‹‹ RESUME PLAY ››

THURSDAY

"May I speak with you, Hester?" Ms. Walker asks. I haven't even dropped my bag at my desk yet.

I lug it with me. My legs are jelly and there's a sinking sensation in my gut. What did I do now?

"Hi," I say. Everyone else rummages through backpacks and notebooks, whispers and giggles.

"Did you complete the video project in conjunction with the letter you wrote me?"

I hate when she uses vocabulary words in everyday conversation.

"Um, yeah," I say. "I sent you the link last night. We had to go out to dinner with my aunt and uncle, and it was so lame, and I had to study for social studies . . ."

She waves her hand, cutting me off.

"I never received it. Do you have it on a thumb drive?"

My knees go weak. Did she just say—

"A what?" I ask, feeling stupid. The late bell buzzes. Usually by now Ms. Walker has taken attendance and started on the day's announcements. Silence from the class. Everyone's staring. Their eyes are like twenty pairs of lasers boring into my back, and my hair and shirt will start smoking soon.

"A thumb drive. You know—" She holds up a memory stick.

"Oh. One of those. Uh, no." There's a sinking feeling in my guts and my chest tightens. "I emailed you the link. Maybe it's in your spam folder?"

Snickers and voices from behind me.

Ms. Walker shakes her head. It's like she's forgotten that there's a bunch of other kids sitting in the room. Meanwhile, I'm standing here, wearing awkwardness like a bad T-shirt.

"Take your seat, Hester. We'll discuss this after class."

I slink to my seat, dragging my bag. Sarah turns all the way around in her chair and studies me like I'm a science experiment. Not what I need right now. Not at all.

"Shut up," I growl at her, even though she wasn't saying anything.

Ms. Walker stands in front of the room and starts talking, but I can't focus on anything she says. Why didn't I put the movie on a memory stick? Why didn't she get the link? I did all that work on Sir Oakheart—and have been wearing long-sleeve tees all week because my elbow is still blue!—and she didn't even see it.

The panic rises through my body. I'm going to fail. *I'm not going to be able to be in the Hoot.* I rub the heels of my hands *hard* against the tops of my thighs.

But if I think like that, I'll end up right back in Mr. Sinclair's office. I have to get it together so I can convince Ms. Walker to accept my project.

Breathe.

Focus.

Count the number of camera angles in the cantina band scene in *Star Wars*.

Slowly, like waves pulling back from the shore, the panic slides away.

Ms. Walker has a list of questions about *The Giver* on the board. I copy them down before she can erase them. I also add "Study for test," but the board doesn't say when the test is and I keep forgetting to ask Max about it.

Ms. Walker calls me over to her desk after class. Kids file past me, and I know they know that I screwed up again. I take a breath and hope I can stay calm.

"Did you check your spam folder?" I ask. My words come out too fast, and sound sharp, like I'm accusing her of something. I snap my mouth closed. *Get it together, Hess.*

She holds up the iPad that all our teachers use. Her school mailbox is open, and although I squint, read really carefully and slowly, and check the list two times, I don't see my name.

"I'm not lying! I sent it!" Heat spreads through me, and the panic ants are not far behind.

"I did not say you were lying." Ms. Walker's words are slow, patient, and very clear, as though she's talking to a child who is throwing a temper tantrum. Is that how she thinks I'm acting? "I am simply pointing out that it's not *here*. And if it's not *here*, I can't give you credit for it."

"What if we log into my YouChannel account? I don't have my phone, but maybe I could do it on your iPad?" *Please please please.*

Ms. Walker sighs impatiently. "Students can't sign in on teachers' technology."

Well, that's a stupid rule. My hands twist together, knotting and unknotting, my frustration out there for her to see. I stuff them in my pockets, but they won't stay put.

I can't remember my strategies.

"I will resend it!" I say, the solution simple. "I just have to borrow a friend's phone to do it." Because of course I left mine at home today.

Ms. Walker shakes her head. "I'm afraid that won't work, Hess. The condition was that it was due in class, today. It's extra credit. I didn't want to offer it, you didn't get it in in time, and I don't have to accept it late. Your other classwork is more important."

"But I spent so much *time* on it!" I can't help it, I'm crying. And I kind of don't care.

Ms. Walker tightens her lips into a line. She hands me a tissue, and I push it away. I sniff snot, hard, into my head. Anger, frustration, and the overwhelming feeling of failure mix in me like a soup of sadness.

"I'm sorry," she says. But I can tell she doesn't mean it.

"Yeah," I mumble. I grab a tissue and head for the door.

A FEW MINUTES LATER

Nev finds me sitting on the sticky hall floor in front of my locker. I plopped down to finish my cry. When I'd stopped, standing up and turning the dial to open it seemed like too much effort.

She offers me a hand, and I take it and clumsily get up.

"What's wrong?" Her usual no-nonsense expression is replaced with concern. My eyes well up again.

"Walker won't accept my extra credit project, even though I totally did it!" I drop my forehead on Nev's shoulder and she hugs me. If this were a movie, we'd team up and figure out a way around Ms. Walker and her rules.

But this is not a movie. Instead, we both know I'm sunk. After a minute, she nudges me toward the girls' bathroom. We aren't supposed to be in the halls during lunch.

I lean against the sinks.

"It's not fair! I sent the link, then she asked if I had it on a memory stick."

"Did you?" Nev crosses her arms and props herself against one of the stalls.

"No," I answer, feeling stupid all over again. "But I sent her the link! Last NIGHT. So she should have had it. I never even thought to put it on a memory stick."

"But the code . . ." Nev furrows her brow, like she's confused that I didn't know about the code.

"I know the stupid code," I snap. Our school has a digital homework code/policy thing, where if you're turning something in electronically, it should be in two forms—email and memory stick, cloud file and memory stick, blah blah.

"We were running late and it didn't seem like I needed it." It sounds lame, and her face tells me she thinks the same thing but is choosing not to say anything. And then I remember—"Hey, do you have your phone? Can I check and see why it didn't go through?"

"Where's yours?" Nev pulls hers from a pocket in her jeans.

"Home." I brush off the question and take her phone.

She hands it over and I dial in her password (*0927*, her birthday) and open the YouChannel app. The stupid tiny keyboard makes logging her out and me in tough. I enter my password twice, afraid it will lock me out if I get it wrong again.

"Come on come on come on," I say to hurry it up. I'm tingly and jumpy.

The bell rings.

"I gotta get my stuff from lunch," Nev says, hand open.

"In a sec." The wheel of access spins. *Lemme in lemme in . . .*

"Hess!"

"I'll bring it to you. In science." My eyes never leave the screen.

Nev sighs. "Put it in my locker," she says, and races out of the bathroom.

My YouChannel appears on the top of the screen. I tap on *My*

Videos and the MK Nightshade piece is at the top. Stupid phone screen is so small I have to scroll to see—

OUTGOING: 1

Wha . . . ??

I tap the box and see: I never clicked SEND. It feels like my blood drains from my body. This whole time, it was just sitting in my account. I click SEND even though it probably won't do any good.

I am glad I'm in the bathroom, because I'm pretty sure I'm going to yurk.

AFTERNOON—SCIENCE CLASS

I get my act together and make it to science before the late bell, but didn't eat lunch. Again. Max thinks skipping meals is pretty much the worst thing ever, and begs me to give him my chips during our lab—"so they don't go to waste."

I hand them over, and he tries to open the bag quietly so Mr. O'Malley won't catch him. I swear, not only can the man hear a crinkling bag from the other side of the lab, he can smell sour cream 'n' onion flavoring from the moon.

"What? No jingle?" Nev says. "You're slipping, bro."

"Nah. I'm saving them now. There's a big contest sponsored by Happy Sprouts frozen vegetables—you know, the ones in the blue-and-orange bag?—and the winner gets free vegetables for a year and a thousand bucks. I'm focusing." Max shoves a full handful of chips into his mouth and chews.

"Free vegetables for a year? I'm not sure I'd want that." I pick at a blue cuticle. "I mean, I like corn and stuff, but doesn't Happy Sprouts only do weird veggies that no one likes? Like beets? And okra."

"I don't care about the vegetables. My dads and Avó can do whatever they want with them."

"Happy Sprout, you've got about three . . . two . . . one . . ."

Nev whispers. Max stuffs nearly the rest of the small bag into his mouth.

"Who has the food?" Mr. O'Malley calls. His small blue eyes scan the class. "You know the drill." He shakes the metal garbage can next to his desk.

Max pours the bits into his mouth and trudges to the front of the room.

I take the opportunity to return Nev's phone. She glares at me. I should've put it in her locker, but I didn't have time. The only thing Mr. O'Malley likes more than ruining snacks is holding on to a kid's phone for the whole day. To get it back he makes you label the organs of a worm—correctly. It's a good thing I'm always leaving my phone at home. He'd have it forever.

"Did you figure out what happened?"

I tell her. Max comes back and we check our liquids and identify if they're an acid or a base with strips of litmus paper. Well, they do most of the checking. I'm passing them the strips.

Nev's eyebrows drop and her nose bunches.

"So, this is awkward, but . . ." she begins.

"What?" My hands are clammy. Max pulls the litmus strips out of them, so I won't trigger a reaction.

"Wellll . . ." Nev draws the word out, like she's trying to figure out how to put the next sentence together. She looks at Max, who slides his eyes to the lab table. He grabs the vinegar and pours some in a petri dish.

"I'm kind of worried. Academic permission forms are due for the Hoot on Monday. Do you think she'll sign yours?"

I scratch at the edge of my lab sheet, picking at the corner.

Suddenly, this paper is super fascinating. I lean closer to the table-top, trying to loosen the tightness in my body.

"Maybe," I mumble. "Probably." The tightness has condensed into a hot, heavy ball in my guts. I am ragged, like the shredded corner of my paper.

I hope so.

‹‹ FAST-FORWARD ››

- Drag through the rest of the school day
- Mom works with me on math. I still can't do it. She gives up.
- Watch *Ghostbusters* instead of doing anything else
- Bed, morning, school. Again.

‹‹ RESUME PLAY ››

FRIDAY

"TGIF!" Nev twitters at my locker like a happy bird. I want to shoo her away. My mood is dark, and Ms. Walker stands between me and my weekend.

"Are you around to work on *The Spy Who Bugged Me*?" I ask. Nev has her duffel bag, which means she's swapping houses. I've lost track of where she's staying this week, because her mom had a business trip and that bounces her schedule around.

"Maybe? I'm with Dad this weekend, but I don't know what his plans are."

If I can keep her talking about the movie, maybe we can both forget that my bad grades might cause a problem with the project.

She says she'll text me, and then Max joins us.

"How's the contest coming?" I ask.

"Okra! Okra! Add it to soup. Let Happy Sprouts vegetables level up your food." He grins wide.

"No," Nev and I say together. He sighs and turns to me.

"Are you ready for the test?"

"Test?" My mouth goes dry. "Which one?" I say, trying to sound like I totally prepared. Nev doesn't buy it.

"Language arts. *The Giver* test," Max answers.

I say a lot of very bad words in my head, but what comes out of my mouth is "Oh, yeah. That one. Totally."

That one that I kept meaning to ask you about. That one that I need to pass. That one. Sure. Yeah, no problem.

"Cool. Good luck!" Nev flits off to leave her duffel in the front office, and I drag down the hall to homeroom like I'm wearing anchors instead of sneakers.

LATER—LANGUAGE ARTS

If this were a movie, language arts would be a bad dream sequence. I'm so anxious and worked up by the time I get in there that colors are extra bright and voices extra loud.

My arch-nemesis, Ms. Walker, stands at the front of the room, talking about the test.

Her voice goes from being too loud to suddenly absent. I focus on her mouth moving—her teeth big and chompy, a dab of spit sits at the corner of her lips. Behind her glasses, her eyebrows move like furry caterpillars. She is no longer a teacher, she's a monster.

And I am *so* not a hero.

Panic threatens to overwhelm me. I drop my head to my desk, squeeze my eyes closed tight.

Calm down calm down calm down . . .

Be Sir Oakheart. Be Black Widow. Be Wonder Woman. Heck, be Miss Piggy. Get it together, Hess!

A bony finger taps on my shoulder, and I jump. She's next to me!

"Your test," she says. She places it on my desk. My heart pounds.

"Can I take it in Mr. Sinclair's office?" The words come out in a whisper. Wonder Woman doesn't whisper. Miss Piggy definitely doesn't whisper. Today, I'm a loser.

Walker's mouth tightens into a line.

"You're supposed to set that up in advance," she says.

I stare at the back of the test sheet. Shrug a little. Around me, kids shift, anxious to get going. If she doesn't let me leave, I'm sunk. I'll have another freak-out. I know this.

She sighs. She may know it, too.

"Fine. Go. Leave your bag here. Be back by the bell."

I don't waste a second. I grab my stubby, teeth-mark-covered pencil and the test, and bolt for the door.

I hope Mr. Sinclair is in his office.

☆   ☆   ☆

His door is open a crack. Relieved, I knock.

"Come in."

I open it wider, stick my head in. Mr. S. is at his desk, papers spread all over it. Sun shining through the light catcher in his window beams blue on his bald spot.

"I have a test from Ms. Walker. Can I take it . . . ?" I trail off. He frowns.

"You're supposed to set that up in advance, Hess." He beckons me to come in. I squeeze through the small opening I've made between the door and the frame.

"I forgot when it was. She wants me back at the end of the period." I glance at the clock. I have less than thirty-five minutes to take the test, which I haven't even looked at.

Mr. Sinclair rubs his eyes. "Fine. Go to Conference Room A

down the hall. And you come and see me on Monday. We need to talk."

"Thank you," I whisper, feeling awful.

Get to the conference room.

I sit down and finally look at the test.

> *1. Describe the trials that Jonas undergoes as he learns about his gift. Be specific.*

> *2. What danger does Sameness pose to the community? Give two examples.*

> *3. What qualities does Jonas develop during his work with The Giver? Name at least two, be specific.*

Forget being a hero, right now I *need* a hero: Sir Oakheart with his sword, Black Widow and her mad skills . . . someone. *Anyone.*

I try. Honest, I do.

But no one comes to save me. I am officially doomed.

FRIDAY LUNCH

For the first time in a while, I am at our table before Nev and Max.
I open my lunchbox and pick at the container of cut-up cucumbers
my dad stuck in there.

Nev plops her stuff across from me.

"How was it?" she asks.

Did it have to be the first thing out of her mouth?

I shrug.

Max joins us. "Was the test bad?"

Did they plan this? I choke down a suddenly slimy, metallic-
tasting cucumber and gulp from my water bottle. My whole body
is heavy with shame and anxiety.

"It sucked," I say, eyes on Iron Man and the Hulk. I try to call
on my heroic idols, but Miss Piggy and friends have turned their
backs on me. I slump in my chair.

Max and Nev exchange glances. Max takes one of my cukes.
He looks like he's about to go off on another jingle idea, but thinks
better of it and just eats.

"Um, but you passed, right?" Nev says the words slowly, with
hope, like she doesn't already know the answer. She keeps her gaze
on the table.

If this were a movie, I'd fake them out and totally have nailed it. Or maybe there would be a massive earthquake and a crack would open in the floor and swallow me whole.

But this is not a movie.

"I took it in Sinclair's office. I didn't finish." My words squeeze out of tiny accordion lungs. I count the seeds in a cucumber slice. I'm at five before either of them speak.

"That sucks." Max sprays Pringles crumbs on the table with each *s* sound. I pry my eyes off the cukes and to his face. The corners of his mouth are turned down. There are Pringle bits on his lips.

Wait—there were Pringles in *my* lunch. Not anymore.

Nev folds her arms on the table and drops her head into them. She peers up at me, just two dark eyes filled with sadness. My stomach shrinks into a tight knot.

"Hess, I don't want to say this. . . ." Her words are muffled by her arms. She tilts her head down again, so I'm looking at the bright part line that zigzags across her hair.

I know what's coming, even though I pretend to myself that I don't.

"We"—*mumble mumble muffle*—"Hoot with you."

"What?" I say, hoping the middle part is something like "can't wait to do the" or "will stand by doing the."

She lifts her head up and props her chin on her stacked arms. "We can't do the Hoot with you," she says. I'll give her credit—she looks at me while she says it.

It's like I've been hit with an arrow in the guts, and I even glance around the caf to see where the bowman must be hiding.

I wrap my arms around my stomach. Max has stopped scarfing my lunch and stares at me with a worried expression.

I try to breathe, but nothing moves in or out. How could they bail on me? I don't know that I failed—only that I didn't finish question two . . . and I never started question three. But still! Ms. W. hasn't corrected it yet. She might totally sign my slip on Monday!

"We don't *know* that I'm out." I manage to choke out the words. Max and Nev exchange a glance. It's like they planned this.

Had they planned this?!?

"It's not personal, Hess," Max says. "We just . . ." He shrugs. "We really want to do it, and the rules say you can only be in one act. We can talk about it at Nev's dad's house tomorrow."

My lips are numb. I wish my heart was, too.

"We can't take the chance," Nev says.

It's her words—those words, *We can't take the chance*, like I'm some messed-up failure—that snap me out of Pain City and into Hulk Mode: The caf noises get a whole lot louder, colors get brighter, and suddenly I. Just. Don't. Care.

"Fine," I say. "Then I can't *take the chance* on working on *The Spy Who Bugged Me* this weekend. Or ever again!" I regret the words as I'm saying them, but who cares?

Nev leans back, eyes wide and surprised. Max's mouth is open. There are Pringles in it.

"C'mon, Hess," Max says, recovering first. "I get it—it sucks. But don't do this."

"Do what?" I say, forcing my words to sound light and fluffy, not like the rocks clacking in my guts. I stuff what's left of my lunch back into my lunchbox so I don't have to look at him. "You guys *did it*, by telling me I'm out of the Hoot. It's my project."

"Seriously, Hess? Is that what you think?" Nev sits straight and stares at me with laser eyes. "You think *we* did this? *You're* the one who's failing everything. *You're* the one who can't pass one test and get a permission slip signed. This will bring us down with you. This is *your* fault. *Not* mine. *Not* Max's."

That "your" smacks me in the heart. I want to hide, or run, or turn them into toads. Instead, I Ultra Hulk Out: brain off, mouth on.

"Don't act so perfect," I snap back without thinking. "Like you're doing me a *favor* by being my friend. Like I'm not the *only* person who talked to you when you joined our class in fourth grade" — kids like Sarah made fun of her name and how smart she is — "and has been your friend ever since. Remember *that*?!"

The hurt look crosses her face and all I can do is push back from the table and get as far away from the caf as possible.

I end up in an empty corner outside of the gym, where I lean my forehead against the wall and hope that the vice principal is done doing rounds and won't find me here.

This is *not* all my fault. It's not. I've *tried* to get stuff done — I mean, I did the extra credit project and it came out awesome — it's not my fault that I can't take stupid tests. Nev knows that my brain is broken, that I can't be as good at stuff as she is. I'm not trying to take anyone down with me.

Right?

« FAST-FORWARD »

- No lab in science; Nev & Max don't even look at me
- Walk home alone
- Text from Nev: Let's forget about lunch . . . but don't forget about tomorrow.
- Watch Indiana Jones movies until I can't stay awake anymore

« RESUME PLAY »

SATURDAY

"Can you take me to the library?" I ask my mom over breakfast.

Dad drops his bagel onto the counter, crosses the room, and puts his good hand across my forehead, like he's checking to see if I am getting a fever.

"Who are you and what have you done with my daughter?" he mocks.

"Dad!" I swat his hand away. "Come on. I have to do some stuff for school."

If I fix up my vocabulary tests and do my reading logs, maybe Ms. Walker will sign that permission slip on Monday.

"Sure," Mom says. "No problem. We can go after lunch."

It's nice out, so to kill time I grab my camera and a hoodie and go to the T station at the end of our street and shoot footage of the trains, then over to the park, where I get some kids playing soccer.

Miss Vogel, the drama teacher, told me a long time ago not to zoom in or get anyone's faces if I didn't have a waiver form for them to sign. Kids, especially—parents get freaked out if there's a stranger shooting their little angel.

When the SD card is full, I go home. Mom's waiting in the kitchen.

She drives and I fiddle with the satellite radio. Mom really loves pop and lite rock, but that's not my scene. We agree on the '80s rock station, though, so I turn it up.

Def Leppard pounds through the car speakers, and we sing along.

"Want to stop at Dunks first?" It's her favorite coffee spot. Most of the time, she gets a latte and I get some frothy chocolate drink that pretends it's a coffee.

No mocha-choca-latta-ya-ya for me today, though. "I don't think so," I say. "I really should get to work."

She pulls into the library parking lot. Turns the car off. Turns to me.

"What's going on, Hess?"

I keep my eyes on my ragged bluish cuticles. I shrug.

"I have work to do."

"I can't remember you ever asking to come to the library." She leans her head against the headrest and puts her hand on the console between the seats, palm up. I want to reach out for it, but I don't. I can't bring myself to, because if I hold her hand, I'm going to feel like a little kid again and start bawling.

"I'm trying to do better in my classes," I say. I don't go any further than that.

"Oh. Of course," she says. "That's great to hear." But I know, and she knows I know, that there's more to it. She waits and I don't say anything else.

"When do you want me to come back for you?"

Suddenly, even though I don't want to tell her everything that's going on, I want her nearby. "Don't you want to pick out a book?"

I catch the slightest hint of a sigh, and then she says, "Of course."

We get out of the car and walk in together.

☆　　☆　　☆

On the way back to the parking lot, Mom's telling me about some commercial that she saw that made her crack up:

"And the song plays, and the wife launches herself at the husband, and—"

And it's like someone dumped a bucket of ice water on my head—and I know what that feels like, because I took that ice bucket challenge when it was a thing and recorded a ton of kids in Nev's Have A Heart Club doing it.

There's an initial shock, and then my whole body, down to my toes, is zapped by ice-lightning.

I am not supposed to be at the library.

I am supposed to be with Nev and Max.

‹‹ PAUSE ››

Okay, let's discuss this: You think I am a total flake.

I get it. I'd think that, too, if I weren't me.

But I can't really explain how crazy easy it is for me to get swept up in stuff, how the only thing that I can focus on is what's right in front of me.

Seriously.

And it's not like the conversation at lunch went well!

So don't be too mad at me, okay? Cut me some slack.

« RESUME PLAY »

MOMENTS LATER

"They are going to be so mad." I take a deep breath, or try to. It gets stuck in my throat and I cough. I didn't even get as much done at the library as I wanted to — all of their copies of *The Giver* were checked out, and I forgot to bring mine from home. I did fix my vocab tests, though.

"Calm down, honey. I'm sure they'll understand."

I want to believe my mom, but I know that they are going to be annoyed. They're already annoyed that we can't show the movie at the Hoot. I'm sure, if I'd had my phone with me, they would have reminded me. They'd probably been texting all day, but the phone was still attached to the charger, somewhere in my room.

"Do you want me to drop you off at Nev's father's house?" Mom asks as we turn down our street.

I gulp, then nod. Probably best to get it over with — if they are even still there. I had no idea if the plan was to get together morning or afternoon. And that makes me anxious.

But Mom's car is in front of the house now, and before I can talk myself out of it, I'm crossing the front lawn. I tap on the door, half hoping no one hears and I can slink home to pretend like nothing happened.

No such luck. It swings open, and her dad gives me a big, then puzzled, grin.

"Hess! So nice to see you. How are you?"

I stammer something in response and he tilts his head.

"I am afraid, though, that Nev and Max aren't here. They left an hour ago and went for ice cream. Would you like me to tell them that you came by? I think they were expecting you."

I take a breath: *onetwothree in, onetwothree out.* "Yes, please," I say. "Tell Nev I'll call her, too."

He closes the door and I race home, dreading what I'm going to find on my phone but knowing that I have to check it.

It's worse than I thought:

> Yesterday 8:20 p.m.
> **N:** See you guys tomorrow, rite?
> **M:** 11:30?
> **N:** Yep. At Dad's. Hess?

And then:

> Today 11:45 a.m.
> **N:** Where you at?

> 11:48 a.m.
> **N:** Hess?!

> 11:50 a.m.
> **N:** WTH?

12:00 p.m.
N: Forget it. Don't come.

I type my apology to them both:

OMG, guys. So so so sorry. Mom took me to the
library. Where are you? Can I still meet you?

I stare at the screen, willing the little notice to change from
Delivered to *Read*.

Finally, it does. My stomach twists and my shoulders are somewhere up by my ears. I try to breathe and relax. Maybe they won't
be mad. Maybe it'll be okay. I wait for the little bubbles that show
you someone is responding.

I wait.

And wait.

But there's no reply.

TWO WEEKS AGO

SUNDAY

Dad's sitting at the table, half an everything bagel in front of him and his forehead scrunched up. He's wearing one of Jack's oversized track hoodies, but one sleeve hangs empty.

"What's up?" I grab a blueberry bagel from the bag on the counter and go in search of garlic cream cheese. Sounds gross, I know, but it's my fave.

He shakes his head. "It's this article . . ." He squints at his phone screen.

"The bakery one?" I take my bagel from the toaster. He nods, not looking at me.

"Can you type yet?"

He shakes his head no. "Not fast enough. The break in my shoulder is high, so I can't rest my right arm on the desk and try to half type with my right hand. I'm one-winged for another couple of weeks, according to the guys in PT. I should've fixed that darn step."

"It's okay," I say, spreading the cream cheese across the blue-purple bagel. "It wasn't your fault."

He puts the phone down and gives me a half smile. "Actually, Hess, it *is* my fault. I'd been putting off fixing the steps because I'd always find something better to do than repair them. And they were dangerous. I guess I should just be glad that it wasn't you or your mom or your brother that fell. Then I'd feel even worse than I do now."

If this were a movie, I'd throw my arms around him and give him a hug. I'd tell him that I'd help, and he'd find a way through it and write the best darn article about that bakery that anyone had ever seen. It'd be sweet and we'd have a "moment."

But I can't say that. I can't help. His forehead scrunches back up.

I take my bagel, about to slip out of the room.

Another look at Dad, chin propped in his good hand, frowning at the table, and I put the bagel on the counter. I step closer to the table.

"Dad?" He turns to me, still frowning, still sad. Without saying anything else, I lean over and give him a kiss on his cheek.

"I'm gonna help you," I say.

He tilts his head.

"Remember? You're taking me to the bakery, to shoot while you interview the owners?"

He grins. "You're right. Get ready." We high-five, and just like that, we make a movie moment.

SUNDAY
AFTERNOON — BAKERY

EXT. Nazari's Bakery. A brick-front building with large windows displaying breads, cakes, and treats. A pair of empty blue window boxes on either side of the door. The door opens.

CUT TO: Bakery interior. Four small café tables and chairs are to the left of the door. Display cases filled with more breads and pastries across the back. Signs offering coffee, hot chocolate, and "light fare" — salads and spreads.

Pan across the display cases, lingering on the pita and loaves of bread, baked to a golden perfection and dusted with flour. Then the tarts, fruit-topped, shiny with glaze.

VOICE
Can I help you?

End scene. Darkness.

Dad steps forward and extends his hand to the short, dark-haired man behind the counter.

"Matthew Greene," he says. "I'm writing the *Weekender* article on your bakery. This is my daughter, Hess."

"Adnan Nazari," the man says. His eyes are warm and he has a dimple in one cheek. "Welcome to Nazari's Bakery!"

"Is it okay if Hess films? We spoke on the phone . . ." Dad trails off, and both men look at his sling.

"Of course!" Mr. Nazari says. "Absolutely."

"Thanks." I click the camera back on and keep one eye on the screen, one eye on where Dad and Mr. Nazari are going.

INT. Bakery. MR. NAZARI comes out from behind the counter.

MR. NAZARI
We opened in February of this year.

DAD
This space used to be a burrito place, right?

MR. NAZARI
Yes. The owners were retiring. My wife and I did all of the work in here.

The men stand next to one of the café tables.

MR. NAZARI

Come in the back. I will show you where we bake.

CUT TO: The kitchen area of the bakery. All of the mixers and appliances are sparkling clean. Ingredients are labeled in bins on shelves, and a big sink off to the side is empty.

MR. NAZARI

This is really a family store. My wife and I take turns
doing the bread in the morning. It's an early
day—four o'clock in the morning. My daughter,
Zada, helps at the register when she is not at school.
Working the register helps all of us with our English.

OFF-CAMERA VOICE
(*mine*)
Your English is very good!

MR. NAZARI

Thank you. We study hard.

I get footage of the ovens, the cooling racks for loaves of bread and other treats, and the prep and baking areas. Then Dad and Mr. Nazari sit down to talk at a small table in the back. I take a small tripod out of my bag and set it on a nearby counter, adjust the zoom, and check the sound. I attach my external mic.

"You're set," I say. "I'll go in the front while you're talking. Just turn the camera off when you're done."

"Oh!" Mr. Nazari hops out of his chair. "I need to get Zada." He crosses the room to a desk tucked in an alcove, and dials his cell phone. He says something in . . . Syrian? Arabic? I don't know what they're speaking—and comes back.

"She'll be right down," he says apologetically. "Sunday afternoons are slow, so she doesn't usually have to work."

I leave Dad and Mr. Nazari to their interview and return to the front of the store. Before I remember that they haven't spoken to me since yesterday's mess, I text Nev and Max pictures of the tarts and bread in the display case. Max would love this place. I zoom in on a strawberry tart.

"Can I help you?" a soft voice says.

I jump. "Sorry," I say automatically.

A girl around my age, her head wrapped in a scarf, is behind the counter. She looks familiar.

"Hi," I say. "I'm Hess. My dad is talking to your dad in the back."

"I'm Zada," she answers. "Do you want anything?"

Well, yeah! "Sure. My dad will pay you when he's done." I look at the case, trying to decide.

"Do you like baklava?" Zada asks. "Mama just made some this morning."

"I've never had it. What is it?"

"Delicious," Zada answers. "Hold on." She disappears into the back and comes back with a big plate of what looks like dessert lasagna—layers of some kind of dough with a glaze and nuts everywhere.

"Try it," she urges, taking a forkful. The dough rustles as the fork breaks through the layers. "My grandmother made the best baklava, but Mama's is good, too."

I stab my fork in the other side of the baklava square. It smells sweet.

"It's honey and nuts and stuff," Zada says, catching me studying my fork.

Things I like. I nibble the edge that's on my fork and am rewarded with a sweet, sticky, crunchy taste. Oh, *heck* yeah. I take a big bite.

"It's good?" Zada asks.

I can only smile and nod, my mouth too full to answer. It's amazing. Max would eat the whole pan. When I'm done, I smile again.

"Delicious!" I say. "Hey, do you go to Howard Hoffer Junior High?"

"I'm a seventh year. No—wait—seventh grader," Zada says.

"I'm in eighth grade." *For the time being*, I think. "I don't see you around school."

"I take ELL classes to learn English and only switch for my art class," Zada answers.

Oh. That explains it. The English Language Learner classroom is down this hall that I never use.

"Your English is very good. I don't think I could move to a new place and learn a language like you're doing."

Zada smiles. "I'm working hard."

And then I remember: Zada was in Mr. Sinclair's office the day that I had the epic panic attack.

"Do you know Mr. Sinclair?" I ask. And as soon as the words leave my lips, I decide that I'm not going to tell Zada about the panic attack. I don't have to be a mess to her right away.

"He helps me sometimes," she says. "He asks me if I'm making friends, and if I'm okay." From the look on Zada's face, I can tell that sometimes she's not okay.

"And," she goes on quickly, "he gave me a secret weapon to help with my English!"

She sees my raised eyebrow and says, "I'll show you." She leaves the table, and I happily devour more baklava. Dad should really bring some of this home. And not tell Jack we have it.

Zada scoots behind the counter and comes back, a stack of books in her hand. She proudly slides them across the table.

Roller Girl. Babymouse. Smile. I flip through them.

"Graphic novels," Zada says. "They help me learn English. I can see the story when I read it and know what the words mean."

I don't say anything. I feel like the floor has opened up under my chair.

"You get to read graphic novels . . . for school?" I can't quite picture Ms. Walker assigning anything to us with pictures. But this is just like storyboarding, and three pages into *Smile*, I'm hooked.

"Yes." She smiles again. "I liked that one. Would you like to borrow it?"

I've been zipping through the book as she spoke. "Um, you don't mind?"

Zada shakes her head. "It's okay. I reread it to study. You can borrow it."

"Thank you so much. I'll take care of it," I say. I haven't been this interested in a book since I started listening to *A Sea of Serpents*.

Dad and Mr. Nazari come out of the back room. Dad has my camera in hand.

"We're all set, honey," he says. I ask him to bring home some baklava, and Zada goes to box it up while Mr. Nazari rings up our order. Zada returns with the baklava.

"Thanks so much," I say. "For the book, too."

"You are welcome," she says. She takes a breath. "I'll see you in school?" she asks, almost like she's afraid of my answer.

"Of course," I say. I like talking to Zada. I make a mental note to go down that ELL hallway this week.

MONDAY MORNING

Nev didn't message me last night, not even to respond to the pho-
tos from the Nazaris' bakery, so I'm not surprised when she doesn't
show up at my locker . . . but I was still kind of hoping she would.
I cram my stuff in there, narrowly avoiding another landslide, and
drag my feet to Ms. Walker's room for homeroom. I didn't sleep
well—I stayed up way too late reading *Smile*—and today I feel
like the undead. To make matters worse, for the first time ever, I've
left my camera at home.

I may as well be naked.

As soon as I cross into homeroom, Ms. Walker waves me to
her desk. Frowning and tight-lipped, she passes me an Office
Appointment slip—but not the regular kind. It's the bright yellow
one that means you're meeting with more than one administrator.
Translation: You're in trouble.

"Don't be late," she says, frown getting even deeper. "After
fifth period."

I nod, feeling too awful to even see who is on the slip, and take
my seat. The morning announcements begin—and of course, the
first one is a reminder that academic permission forms for the
Hoot are due by the end of the day.

"A yellow office slip?" Sarah, in front of me, pretends to be looking for something in the bag on the floor next to her desk. Her long, dark hair acts as a shield between her words and Ms. Walker. "Way to go."

The words land in my heart like knives hitting a target.

She grabs a pen and straightens, her hair sliding across the top of my desk like it's straight out of a shampoo commercial. It takes all the strategies I have not to pull it.

"Shut up," I say.

"No talking during morning announcements, Miss Greene," Ms. Walker says, but she's looking at her phone, and my anger grows even hotter.

I spend the last ten minutes of homeroom *one-two-three* breathing, and wondering how bad the rest of the day will be.

☆　　☆　　☆

Two periods later, I'm back in Ms. Walker's room for language arts. I slip my corrected vocabulary tests—three weeks late, but they're done!—into the Finished Work basket on her desk.

"The end of the marking period is in two weeks," she says to the class, "so if you are missing any assignments or have to make up work, you have until next Friday to do so. Then my grade book is closed and we start fresh for the last portion of the year."

I almost snort out loud. *Starting fresh?* Ha! That would be nice, but that's not really how it works. Especially with Ms. Walker.

She tells us that our last test on *The Giver* is next week—aren't we done with this book yet?—and then she takes a stack of papers off her desk.

"These are last week's tests. I'll hand them back to you at the end of the period." She taps them and puts them back. "If you have any questions regarding where you stand, please let me know. We can go over my grade book together."

We get a list of new vocab words. Then talk about *The Giver*.

Just give the tests back. Just give the tests back, I think. My brain is stuck on a loop, and nothing is getting through it. Finally, with five minutes left in the class, she grabs the tests again.

"Most of you did very well," she says. She holds the pile casually, like it's junk mail or a section of newspaper.

Chills run up and down my back. My armpits are a swampy mess. I *one-two-three* breathe. I think about Black Widow, Miss Piggy, and Wonder Woman. The panic ants crawl out of my socks anyway. I jiggle my legs. Breathe more.

She's still talking.

Pass them out! I want to shout. Even though I know I didn't do a good job—I couldn't have, because I didn't finish—a tiny part of me hopes that I did *enough*. Enough to pass. Enough to have something to feel good about. Enough to pretend that the slip in my bag is not bright yellow.

Finally, she starts moving down the rows, handing back the tests.

"Nirmal."

"Javvy."

"Allie."

And this is worse than the waiting. Because soon I'm going to *know*.

My armpits are sopping wet. Ms. Walker stops next to Sarah's desk, hands her her test.

Then, me.

"Hester." She puts the test facedown on my desk, and says, "Stay after class, please," before she moves on.

I have déjà vu. Only this time, I'm panicking too much to even move. I'm rooted to my chair, and a part of my brain wonders if I'll simply have to stay here for the rest of the day. The green marker shadows through the paper.

My throat squeezes down to the size of a straw. My *one-two-three* breaths are more like *one-two-three* wheezes.

Black Widow, I am not.

My hand shakes a little when I bring it up from my lap to the paper. Can I even turn it over? I'm kind of aware of my classmates packing up and leaving—the bell must have buzzed—and then Ms. Walker is in the empty desk beside me.

Focusing on her is just as bad as the test. I don't know where to look.

"Hester," she says. "Hess." I turn to her.

Her frown is deep, and she tucks her hair behind her ears.

"What happened?" she says.

Those are the worst words she could have said. I haven't even turned the test over, and I know. I *know*.

I will not cry.

I shrug.

She turns the test over for me.

There's a big green NC on it—No Credit. I don't read any of the other words. Why bother? Those two say it all.

"Hess," she says. "We have a problem. Mr. Sinclair and I are going to talk with you about this today."

"What is it?" My voice is a dry croak. I swallow what feels like a mouthful of pencil dust, and try again. "What is the problem?"

"Well." Ms. Walker seems like she doesn't want to say any more. Her eyes dart around the room, like she's the one looking for an escape.

Maybe we could both leave and pretend this never happened? Under my desk, my sneakers rub together, doing a nervous dance on their own. The rubber edging around the sole thwaps loudly in the room.

She takes a breath and tries again.

"You aren't doing well in social studies and math as well, right?"

I nod, my head feeling too heavy for my neck. "I'm going to summer school for those," I whisper. "It's all planned."

"Well, Hester, I'm afraid the district doesn't allow students to take three courses for summer school. And you are not on track to pass language arts." She pauses, and my stomach, which has puddled somewhere around my shoes, drops even lower.

"Which means you are not on track to pass eighth grade."

If this were a movie, she'd offer me a wide grin and say, "*Kidding!*" with a slap on the back. We'd laugh and leave together.

But this is not a movie, and Ms. Walker watches me closely, as though I could explode at any moment.

I might.

Instead, I nod my head. A little one, which is all I can manage.

"We will discuss this more after fifth period. Are you okay?"

That is a very stupid question. But I just nod again.

She slips out of the desk next to mine, I fumble for my bag, and stand on jellyfish legs.

"Hester," she says, and I freeze, but don't turn to look at her.

"I am concerned that you haven't made any progress," she says, like she didn't just drop a bomb on me, like everything is the same as it was at the beginning of the period. "And I would like you to take these packets home and complete them for me, so we can make sure you're comprehending material appropriately." She comes into my field of vision holding another stack of papers—a bunch of packets, stapled together. She holds them out to me, and I automatically take them.

"Please go through them by the end of the week."

I nod again, and move to leave.

This time, I make it out of the classroom.

And that's when the tears come.

SECONDS LATER

A fat tear rolls down one of my cheeks, and as I'm about to run away and find a dark hole to hide in for the rest of my life, Max appears at my side.

"Hey, Hess, you okay?" He doesn't wait for me to answer, which is good, because I definitely can't. "Oh, hey, what're you doing with those? My brother did these for homework last fall. Funny, huh?"

Max's brother is in fifth grade. I am pretty sure that this is the most humiliating moment of my life.

"Gotta go," I say, and I do it. Run away. Leave Max in my dust.

Feet slamming against the hallway floor, dodge kids on their way to lunch, kids at their lockers, kids headed to class. Crash into the science wing's girls' bathroom, and nearly fall over a yellow wet-floor sign. A terrible smell makes it past my snot-filled nose.

"Out of order!" yells Mr. Robertson, the custodian.

Back out, vision blurry and heart pounding. Shaking. Where can I go? Mr. Sinclair's office is my usual spot, but today I don't want anything to do with him or his strategies. They don't help.

Hug the stupid packets to my chest, and, bag banging at my side, take off toward the gym. I just need to be alone.

But as I get closer, there's a crowd. The girls' track team is having a fund-raiser or something, and a bunch of kids are sitting all over the floor, eating cookies and brownies.

Detour down the nearest hall—the arts wing. There, on the right: the AV equipment closet. Miss Vogel showed me where it was last year when I needed a charger for my camera.

Don't be locked don't be locked don't be locked . . .

I bang into the door, twist the knob, and nearly fall into the dark space. Scrabbling against the wall for a light switch, I sink to the ground in front of metal shelves holding DVD players, cameras, and loads of wires, and close the door when the overhead light flickers on.

And then I cry.

And cry.

And cry.

The tears pour out of me like I'm trying to flood the place.

It sinks in: I'm failing eighth grade. I'm not going to be able to go to high school. My friends will move on and be gone.

I suck back snot, trying to breathe.

Now the Hoot won't be the only thing I miss. Add to that list the eighth-grade cruise, the end of the year party, and the move-up ceremony where parents send in stupid pictures of their kids to show in a slideshow . . .

Oh no. My *parents*. The Shame Pit that I'm in gets even deeper.

I've lost it. Deep, shaky sobs roll through my chest. How did I get here?

I've tried. I really have.

Haven't I?

And then . . . images pop into my head of skipping homework to watch Indiana Jones. Crossing out items on my to-do list without even starting them . . . not opening *The Giver*.

I pull my legs even tighter against my body, fold my arms on top of my knees, put my head down.

I'm in a deep well of awfulness—the depths of Mount Doom, the training cave in *The Empire Strikes Back*, and all of Freddy Krueger's nightmares—all rolled into one. And there's no way out.

This sends me into a fresh round of crying. My insides hurt with the force of the sobs, and I have nothing to wipe my nose with, so I use the hem of my shirt. The bell ending lunch rings. I'm supposed to go to science, with Nev and Max . . . and then my meeting with Ms. Walker and Mr. Sinclair.

The late bell buzzes. I cry some more.

I am never leaving this closet.

STILL IN THE CLOSET

I am cried out. My head aches and my eyes feel like overstuffed beanbags. The spot above my upper lip is raw from rubbing with my shirt hem tissue, and my knees creak when I finally straighten them out. I lean my head against the metal shelves behind me and close my eyes.

If this were a movie, I'd fall asleep and be transported into a dream sequence. Maybe it'd be a good dream: one that would give me clues that would help me solve my problem. Or it could be a nightmare: one where Ms. Walker, my parents, and Mr. Sinclair turn into crazy monsters who chase me down the halls of the school. Either way, when I woke up there would be a way out of this mess.

But this is not a movie. I stay still, head back, my insides raw from sobbing, and instead of trying to think of a way out of this situation, I try to pretend that it's not happening. I try not to think of anything. My only plan is to stay here, basically forever.

The door opens. Someone gasps.

My eyes open and my head snaps forward. Tall, thin Miss Vogel stands frozen in the doorway, one hand over her heart and the other extended to the turned-on light switch. Her mouth is open in an exaggerated O.

"You scared me!" she says after a second. "You're not supposed to be in here."

I don't say anything. I can't.

"Is everything all right?" she asks. She steps into the small room, crouches down to my level, and puts a hand on my shoulder.

I shake my head. Everything is definitely *not* all right.

My face must look as swollen and red as it feels, because she stands up, extends a hand, and says briskly, "I don't know where you're supposed to be right now, but you're coming with me."

I don't move. I'm still not sure I can.

"Come on. This is my free period."

I let her help me up and follow her to a tiny office behind the theater classroom. She clears a pile of scripts off a chair next to her desk and tells me to sit down, then hands me a box of tissues. I blow my nose for real a few times.

"What class should you be in, Hess?"

"Science." My raspy throat docs still work, after all.

She uses the walkie talkies that all teachers carry to notify the office that I'm not MIA, then disappears into the classroom and comes back with a small plastic cup of water. It slides down my throat, and my body's jangled, pulled-apart sensation is replaced by a rolling wave of exhaustion.

"What happened?" she asks, concern and worry all over her face. "Do you need help?"

It takes a few seconds, but I realize what she's asking me: Am I safe, has someone hurt me? I gulp some more water and shake my head.

"I'm okay. Nothing bad happened." She rubs her eyes under her glasses and her face relaxes just a little.

Well, that's a lie, but I have no idea how to tell this story. Where do I start? How do I not freak out again when I tell it?

"Take a breath," she says. I breathe. My eyes get all watery again and a black void of hurt opens in my chest. I dab my eyes with a tissue and struggle against going into that sobbing dark place again.

"I'm failing," I say. "Everything."

And it's like a gate lifts inside of me and I tell her all of it: how I wanted to do the Hoot so bad, the unsent email to the extra credit movie that I spent so much time on, failing *The Giver* test, being told that I wasn't going to pass eighth grade, getting fifth grade homework to do . . .

"And now I have to go to a stupid meeting with Mr. Sinclair and Ms. Walker so they can all tell me how much I suck!" Tears run down my cheeks, but I'm too wiped out to care. I just blot and blow and wait for Miss Vogel to tell me how I've made bad decisions and everything is all my fault and I should stay in eighth grade forever because clearly I can't handle high school.

"This is just terrible. I'm sorry, Hess. I really am."

Her words surprise me as much as when Jack dropped an ice cube down my back at a barbecue at the pool last summer. I sit up straight and immediately stop crying. Teachers don't usually say they are sorry. Or that things are terrible.

She takes her glasses off. Her face seems younger without them. She rubs her eyes again and sighs. The wall clock makes a soft electric buzz. Then she props her elbows on her desk and her chin on her hands, and looks straight at me.

"Look, I probably shouldn't say this, so don't spread it around, okay? But lots of creative people struggle with learning—you already know that. There is no one-size-fits-all way to teach people. And no one-size-fits-all way to learn. You're struggling now, but once you get everything you need in place, it will be much easier."

I want to believe her, I really do. But I have Mr. Sinclair's strategies. And my mom's methods. And nothing seems to be working. But she's trying to be helpful, so I force a small smile.

She sees right through it.

"Yeah, you're right," she continues. "Not helpful. Okay. Well, I have to take you to Mr. Sinclair's office so you can have your meeting, but . . . I'd like you to come to Hoot rehearsal tomorrow."

"But I'm not in it," I say.

"I know," she replies. "But there's someone coming who I want you to meet. Will you try?"

I nod and agree to come, even though the Hoot is the last thing I should be caring about.

She fishes through her desk and takes out a package of face wipes, then offers it to me. Grateful, I pull out the sheet and swab my cheeks and eyes with its coolness. I'm sure I still look bananas, but at least I'm not as sticky.

On the way to Mr. Sinclair's office, she has me stop into the girls' bathroom to blot at my now crusty and gross T-shirt. I splash water on my face and avoid looking at myself in the scratched mirror. If I look half as bad as I feel, everyone will be terrified.

We stand outside of Mr. Sinclair's door.

"You ready?" Miss Vogel asks.

Inside, I say, *No*.

Outside: "I guess."

She knocks.

MONDAY—
MR. SINCLAIR'S OFFICE

Walking into his office, I am suddenly aware of the missing weight of my camera. I want its comforting bulk at my hip. I wish I were watching all of this through a lens instead of living it.

Mr. Sinclair sits behind his desk and he gestures to the red squashy chairs. I sink down, glad that he and Miss Vogel step out to talk to each other. Miss Vogel is probably telling him about my AV closet breakdown, and you know what? I don't even care.

When he comes back in, his mouth is turned down in a tight frown. Is he mad at me for ditching class?

"Hess, are you okay?" His face softens and I can tell that it's not me he's mad at.

I nod and rub my eyes. I'm so tired, everything feels heavy.

"Your parents are coming in shortly. Why don't you rest until they get here. We have a lot to discuss, and it seems that the morning took its toll on you."

Wait—*my parents*?!

But I can't even worry about that now. Relieved that he's not making me talk about my feelings, I curl my knees to my chest and close my eyes.

"Hess?"

What seems like a second later, Mom's voice wakes me up. A line of drool stretches from the corner of my mouth, and I swipe it away, embarrassed. Was I snoring, too?

I rub my eyes. "Hey, Mom." She's wearing the black pants and sweater she had on for work today, and Dad's here, too. He gives me a small smile, like the one he gives me when I'm home sick with a stomach bug and feeling like death. Why are they at—

Then it comes flooding back in a rush. They're here because I'm a failure.

Immediately, shame covers me. I stare down at my hands. My blue cuticles are red from picking at them. My hands twist in my lap.

"Come here," Mom says gently. I don't want to. The bell rings, signaling the end of fifth period.

She comes to me instead, wrapping me in an awkward hug on the squishy chair. I hug her back, hard.

"I'm so sorry," I say into her neck. She smooths my hair.

"Don't be," she says. "We'll figure it out."

I climb off the chair on stiff legs, and Dad squeezes me against his side with his good arm.

Mr. Sinclair peeks around the doorframe.

"Are we ready?" No one answers. "Follow me."

We go down the hall to the meeting room where I took that awful *Giver* test. Ms. Walker is already sitting at the table, a stack of papers in front of her. Everyone says hello and I keep my eyes on the blank surface of the table. I don't sit down until Mom puts her hand in the small of my back and guides me to a chair. My parents sit on either side of me, and I'm grateful.

Ms. Walker begins. She tells them my test scores. Shows them her grade book. Tells them that I don't seem to be engaged in class. They talk about my executive function disorder. My anxiety

I want to shrink into a ball and roll away. They are talking about me like I'm not even here, so why bother staying? I count and breathe and sit very, very still.

". . . Right, Hester?" Ms. Walker said something that I'm supposed to answer, I guess.

"Um, can you repeat that?" For the first time, I get a good look at her. She seems grumpy, like she's annoyed that she has to go through all of this.

She frowns, and gives my parents a look like, *See what I mean?*

"I gave you some other assessment work to do this week?" She turns to my parents and Mr. S. "I'm thinking maybe there's more here than what's been diagnosed. Perhaps Hester needs some new strategies, or other ways we can help her."

It's taking all of the strategies I have to not bolt.

Mr. Sinclair leans his elbows on the table. "There's always more to try, but I think what we're seeing here is that Hess is overwhelmed by the frequency of the exams, and not putting in time at home."

My parents nod.

"Things have been hectic around the house lately," Mom says, gesturing to Dad's arm, "and we haven't been as on top of her schoolwork as we usually are. We can all do better here."

"Well, let's do that," Ms. Walker says crisply. "Hester is in serious danger of not passing eighth grade at this point. The marking period closes next week, and we can have another conversation at that time, with the assistant principal, about Hester's eligibility for high school."

A rock sets into my stomach. Next to me, Mom stiffens.

"Of course," she says. "And what options does Hester have at this point for raising her grade in your class?"

Ms. Walker shakes her head, her mouth tiny and tight. "We have one more quiz on *The Giver*, and a vocabulary test. Even perfect scores on both won't move the needle much, I'm afraid."

Mom nods. "I see."

"There has to be something she can do," Dad says. "An extra assignment?"

Ms. Walker barks out a short laugh. "Extra? That didn't go well before. I think she's got enough to handle with what she's been assigned. Don't you?"

Mom and Dad look at me, two sets of surprised faces. I shrug. I never told them about what happened with the Sir Oakheart video. Things just got too crazy with Dad's shoulder.

"We will work on things at home with Hess, and will be in touch with Mr. Sinclair about her progress and strategies," Mom says. "We're concerned, but sure there is a way to get her where she needs to be."

Ms. Walker and Mr. Sinclair set up a follow-up conversation, and then everyone says their good-byes. I still sit at the table, alone. Mr. Sinclair pulls my parents aside, and they talk some more.

"Come on, Hess." Dad appears by my side, bumping me with his sling.

"Huh?"

"We're taking you home."

About. Time.

<< FAST-FORWARD >>

- Awkward ride home, no one speaks
- Listen to *A Sea of Serpents* in my room until dinner
- Act invisible at the table

<< RESUME PLAY >>

MONDAY NIGHT

After dinner I clear my plate without being asked and take Dad's, too. Jack has disappeared to study for a Spanish test, and I'm hoping I can sneak up to my room with no one noticing.

"Come back in here when you're done," Mom calls over the sound of the rushing water. I freeze. What are my escape options?

1. Jet out the back door and run to Nev's dad's house

2. Pretend I didn't hear her and sneak back up to my room, and fake sleep if they come looking for me

3. Put Mom's metal-trimmed mug in the microwave and duck

Unfortunately, none of these are good. I sigh, splash my face with water, and call on Miss Piggy, Wonder Woman, and Black Widow to get me through.

I trudge to the table. Dad points to my chair.

"Well," he begins. "That was a rotten day, huh?"

You could say that, I think. I don't say anything out loud. I'm afraid I'll start crying again, and I am tired of tears today.

"We want to help you," Mom says. I nod, bite my lip, and watch my hands twist and scrape at my cuticles. I don't trust myself to speak.

There's silence. I guess they expected me to cry, or yell, or at least answer. I am sure they're looking at each other, unsure of what to say next.

"Look up here, Hess," Dad says. His face seems older and tired, and I'm sure his shoulder hurts. He takes a breath and sighs. "We need to figure this out."

"There is nothing to figure out. I'm failing. I'm not going to high school," I say.

Mom covers one of my hands with her own. Her nails are cut short and filed round. She doesn't wear nail polish or anything, and I can't help but notice how she doesn't bite them, how pink and smooth and whole they are.

It's kind of like her: She's smooth, never frazzled, never rushed, always calm. I'm so *not that*. I'm all jangles and ants and rushing and panic and mess. And then I wonder, maybe for the first time: *What does she think when she looks at me? How am I her daughter?*

A spot opens inside me, and I want to just fall into myself until I become as small and as dense as a black hole.

But I already am that black hole—sucking everything around me into my disastrous mess. I've pulled in Nev and Max, my teachers, Mr. Sinclair, and now my parents. Every one of them has been caught in my gravity.

And with all these people who love me, if they can't help me get it together, who will?

Mom squeezes my hand and I'm totally in danger of crying again. For once, I'm glad my camera isn't around. No one needs to see this, ever.

"I'm sorry," I whisper, because I don't know what else to say. My chest feels like it's going to burst with the effort of holding back tears. "I've ruined everything."

"You haven't ruined anything," Mom says firmly. She lowers her head to peek under my hair and make eye contact. Her face is set with determination. "You just need more help."

"I don't *want* more help!" I am so very tired of help and strategies. "It doesn't do any good. And even if I do get enough help—whatever that is—to graduate eighth grade, this is going to happen all over again in high school. Only worse, because it's high school." I pull away from Mom's hand.

Mom furrows her brow and glances at Dad. Somehow, I know. I know what's coming is not going to be good.

"This is serious business, Hess. We need you to focus. And for you, focusing means getting rid of distraction." She takes a breath. "Dad and I are going to hold on to your camera for a little while. Just until we get over this hump."

My body turns icy, then heat rushes through me. My brain can't process this, but my guts sure can. They squeeze with pain.

"No," I say, and shake my head. "That's not right. That's not fair. I didn't do anything *wrong*!"

"It's not a punishment," Dad says. "It's the opposite. We just want you to be free to do what you need to do."

"This is not freedom. This is *jail*. This is cutting off my arm. Why would you do this to me?" My voice is really loud and the panic ants swarm up my legs and then my breath locks up. I don't even care. I push back from the table and make a break for the stairs. My parents' faces pass in a blur of sadness.

Mom calls for me, but Dad tells her to leave me alone. I kick the door shut and throw myself on my bed.

If this were a movie, my parents would come after me, talk gently to me, rub my back. There'd be hope that tomorrow would be better and that we could find a solution.

But this is not a movie.

I gasp and breathe short puffs of air.

No one comes.

TUESDAY

I wake up to my alarm, still in my clothes. My body aches like I've slept on rocks instead of my covers.

When I drag myself downstairs, everyone is gone. Mom and Dad left a note about a physical therapy appointment for Dad's shoulder. Jack is nowhere to be found. Maybe he's still asleep—sometimes he doesn't hear his alarm—but I don't bother to check. He can deal with whatever happens if he sleeps all day.

I walk to school alone. Without my camera, it's a flat, bland walk. I don't want to look around, because why bother? I can't capture it. I can't use it.

I don't spot Nev or Max in the hall. I miss them like I'd miss my shadow. For a second, I wonder how their new Hoot project is coming. For a second, I wish I had told them everything—just how bad I'm failing, how I want to get out of it but I am so scared that I can't—but I don't even know where to begin. It's my own stupid fault. Why would they want to talk to a loser?

In language arts, Ms. Walker greets me with a careful hello. I take my seat and don't say anything.

She starts the period talking about the "emotional disconnect" in *The Giver*, and I don't even bother pretending to take notes.

This morning has been about a thirty on the horrible scale. If it were a movie, Rotten Apples would give it a five. Probably a two.

Ms. Walker drones on about "the importance of highs and lows." To distract myself, I dig through my book bag.

The loose handouts, folders, and books float on a sea of paper clips, bits of paper, rubber bands, and pennies. Sticky grit coats my fingertips. There's a flash of bright green. Gum.

"Looking for something, Miss Greene? Your book, perhaps?" Ms. Walker stands at the head of my row, hands on her hips. "We can wait until you find it."

I sigh. "No," I mumble, sticking the gum into the outside pocket and hanging the bag over the back of my chair. I rub my hands together and crumbs patter onto the desk.

Sarah, in front of me, snickers.

The sound shoots through me like a bolt of angry lightning. Like all the disappointing conversations and bad news have morphed into an electron-zapping ball of Supervillain Creation Goo.

If this were a movie, I'd be glowing green right now.

Rage—hot, bubbly, and dangerous—simmers in me. Sarah's long dark hair brushes the top of my desk. And I want to do something to get her, and my parents, and Ms. Walker, and even Mr. Sinclair, back. I want it *so bad*.

My hands are clenched. I open them. My fingers ache from squeezing so tight.

Sarah shifts, and her hair sweeps by again.

I lean back in my seat, trying to keep enough control not to get sent to the principal's office, drop my arms to my sides, and shake out my hands. It doesn't help me relax, but when my fingers brush my bag, I remember the gum.

As carefully as I can, I reach into the outside pocket, keeping my eyes on Ms. Walker the entire time. There's one piece in the package, and I unwrap it in the bag and sneak it into my mouth. Minty explosions help me breathe better, clearing some of the fog of rage.

Chew. Breathe. Chew. Breathe.

I puff out a gust of air, trying to relax. Sarah's hair moves the teensiest bit. Her shoulders hunch up like I've just Big Bad Wolf'ed her straw house.

And then:

She turns, flipping her hair over to the far side of her face—blocking Ms. Walker's view.

"You have always been such a disaster," she hisses through clenched teeth. "A total mess-up, Hess. I can't believe we were ever friends." She straightens in her chair.

And just like that, the rage is back. This time, I let it fill me, infecting every cell in my body. I am Dr. Bruce Banner, Hulking out.

Her hair sweeps my desk again.

Her *hair*.

The anger rises to the point where I can't see, I can't think, I'm not *me*.

And when I get it together, and I can see, and I can think, and I am me again, there's a piece of bright green gum folded into Sarah's long, black, lustrous, hair.

And I smile.

LUNCH

The bell rings, and I bolt out of Ms. Walker's class.

Hess and Satisfying Acts of Revenge: 2

Good Ideas: 0

Oh, great. Max and Nev are waiting at my locker. We haven't talked since I blew them off on Saturday, and they have no idea about my closet meltdown or impending disaster. I push thoughts of Sarah's hair aside. Breathe.

"What's up?" Max asks.

A million things. I'm failing. I just put gum in Sarah's hair. I'm not going to high school.

Instead, I say, "I'm sorry." My eyes fill with tears. "I'm *really* sorry about Saturday."

They exchange glances. Nev sighs. "We know, Hess. It's okay, kind of."

"But it was annoying," Max says.

"I know." I have nothing else to offer. I want to tell them everything, but it seems so hard — there's *so much* ground to cover. So I say nothing.

I stuff my books in my locker and grab my lunch. "Let's go sit down."

Nev peers at me with her all-seeing eyes. "Somethin' else ain't right with you, girlfriend."

I shrug. "The only thing that ain't right is that I'm starving." I can tell she doesn't believe me, but she lets me go to lunch without any more complaining.

It happens when we're sitting at the table. I'm begging Max to do his impression of his math teacher, and there's a bunch of activity on the far side of the room, near Sarah's table. If I had my camera, it'd look like this:

INT. School cafeteria.

Lunch going on as normal. Except at one table. Loud chatter, then silence. Then, as a group, five girls get up and walk to the door, surrounding one protectively.

GIRL AT NEARBY TABLE
What happened? What's going on?

GIRL FROM GROUP
(shakes head, points to her hair)

Zoom to center of the group. Tight shot. It's SARAH.

A sharp shove against my shoulder, and I rock to the side, nearly spilling my water bottle.

"Nev!" I didn't have to look to know it was her. The noise level of the caf goes back to normal. "What'd you do that for?"

"Do you really need to ask?" she says in this really pointed way. I frown at her.

"What do you mean?"

"You tell me. She sits in front of you in Walker's class, doesn't she?"

Max looks from one to the other of us, like we're in a tennis match. Then his eyes go wide.

"Dang, Hess. That's cold. Why?"

I push back from the table. "Why do you think *I* had anything to do with it? We don't even know what happened!" I stand and grab my book bag. "Nice friends."

My stomach churns and my fingers tingle. I'm sure my face is the color of a fire engine. I hate lying. Nev just sits there, shaking her head real slow, and the disappointment on Max's face makes my heart want to melt with shame.

I stomp away from the table, feeling worse with every step. What I did was wrong, and Sarah didn't deserve it . . . except she kind of did. Everyone who's been ragging on me deserves it; Sarah was just the one to get it.

I push the thoughts out of my head by reciting the order of Alfred Hitchcock movies: *Dial M for Murder. Rear Window. To Catch a Thief. The Trouble with Harry* . . .

I'm up to *The Birds* when I realize that I'm standing in front of the library. I've been spending a lot more time here lately. Mrs. Coe told me that she was working on getting some more DVDs added to the collection. There's still time left in the lunch period, and Nev and Max won't come looking for me. I go in.

Our library is pretty small, but there are a lot of books and magazines crammed in it. The shelves are low, and Mrs. Coe got a place at the mall to donate some furniture, so there are squashy chairs and a bunch of tables. Nothing matches, but that's cool.

A girl with a dark blue headscarf is hunched over one of the tables.

"Zada?"

She turns, startled. "Hess! Hello," she says. "What are you doing here?"

Avoiding my friends, I want to say. Instead I answer: "Looking for something. Thank you for letting me borrow your book," I say, remembering. "I don't have it with me, but I will bring it to you."

"Okay," Zada answers. "I actually have a few more in my bag." She hands them to me.

"*El Deafo?*" I laugh at the name.

"It's good," Zada says. I like the cover, with a superhero bunny-person flying past a cloud. She says I can borrow it. Then she goes back to work, and I go to see the librarian.

She's at her desk, eating an apple and reading, of course. *See You at Harry's* must be a good book, because she doesn't even look up until I'm standing in front of her.

"Oh! Hi, dear," she says. She calls everyone "dear." It's so librarian. Her face is blotchy and red, like she's been crying. She blots her face with a tissue.

"Are you okay?"

She blows her nose, blots again.

"Fine. It's this book . . . it's fine. What can I do for you? Can I help you find something?"

"Have you gotten any new DVDs in?" I am jangly and awkward, not sure of where to look and embarrassed that I've interrupted her.

She's nice about it, though. She walks me over to the DVD shelf. "The administration isn't crazy about me stocking these, so I don't broadcast the new stuff the same way I do for books. But there are a few things in here that you might like." She pulls out a documentary on the making of a bunch of sci-fi and fantasy movies. MK Nightshade's *A Sea of Serpents* movie is one of the ones listed on the case. Next she shows me the latest action movies that have come in. As soon as I thank her, she flies back to her book and I go on pretending that everything is fine.

I've seen the action movies, but the DVDs have some cool extras — interviews with the director, some special effects explanations — and I decide to take one of them out.

I leave the fantasy/sci-fi documentary on the shelf and say good-bye to Zada on my way out.

Weirdly, instead of watching the movie, I kind of want to finish the *Sea of Serpents* audiobook.

STILL TUESDAY— BEFORE SCIENCE

A hand taps me on the shoulder as I'm walking to science, and I nearly hit the ceiling it scares me so bad.

"Sorry, Hess!" It's Miss Vogel, carrying a big pile of stapled packets. "Just wanted to remind you—rehearsal is after sixth period!"

I'd forgotten, and there's no way I want to go.

"Oh, yeah," I say. Kids swarm to class around us, trying to beat the bell. A big, clumsy seventh grader knocks into Miss Vogel and she loses her balance a little. Some of the packets fall.

"I got 'em," I say. "Can I carry some stuff for you? Help you out?"

"Oh, thanks," she answers. "But I don't want you to be late for class after missing yesterday."

I want to be late for class, so I don't have to talk to Nev and Max.

"It's okay," I say, grabbing a few more packets to ensure my lateness, "Mr. O'Malley won't mind if you give me a note."

We walk to her office without saying anything. I put the packets on the corner of her desk and wait for her to write out the late slip.

"You're still coming to rehearsal today, right?" she asks as she tears it off the notepad. She holds on to it, waiting for my answer.

"Uhhh, well . . ." I don't want to be rude, but right now the only thing I think I should be doing is digging a tunnel to another school system.

"Say that you'll come," she says firmly. She holds the slip out of my reach, like she won't give it to me unless I agree.

"Fine. Sure." I take the late pass.

"There's someone coming who I really think you'll want to meet," Miss Vogel says casually. She shuffles some papers on her desk, like she's all laid-back and doesn't care if I come or not. I am not going to fall for that. "Someone really interesting."

"Okay. I'll try to be there." I head to science, slip into my seat, and avoid eye contact with Max and Nev. Mr. O'Malley is talking about acids and bases again.

Who could Miss Vogel think that I'd *really want to meet*?

TUESDAY
HOOT REHEARSAL

I don't decide to go until I get there. My feet stop outside of the auditorium, and a few kids squeeze past me to get in the doors. I step to the side and go to dig out my camera, like I have five million other times today.

Ha-ha. It's somewhere in Dad's office.

"Hess?" It's Nev.

"Hey," I say, just as surprised as she looks. "Um, hi." My face gets hot.

"What're you doing here?" She is all business and frowns, and it hurts my heart. I screwed up again at lunch. I so badly want to tell her about how bad everything's gotten, how Miss Vogel wants me here, and how much of an idiot I was earlier, but the words won't come.

Instead, I shrug. "Just . . . you know. Checking it out."

"So you got in?" She crosses her arms and frowns. "You didn't tell us?"

"No. Of course not."

"So you're spying? We want it to be a surprise."

"No! I didn't even think of that. Miss Vogel wanted me here for some reason . . ." I trail off.

"For *what* reason?"

"Um . . . because she wanted me to see it." I don't know where to go with this that doesn't lead to me getting left back. And I definitely don't want to have that conversation here, while kids stream past us into the auditorium.

She cocks her head at me, her long ponytail hanging to one side. She waits. I wait. I don't know what else to say. Finally, she pushes past me, a cloud of annoyance left behind.

I turn to take off when Miss Vogel and a teacher-aged guy that I've never seen before show up. Miss V.'s carrying that same stack of packets, her frizzed-out hair is everywhere, and she's smiling really big.

"Hess! Oh! I didn't see you there," she cries. The packets fall.

The guy helps her pick them up.

"Hess, this is who I wanted you to meet. Professor Crabbe, from Chestnut College. He teaches in the department of theater and film. He's a filmmaker."

A filmmaker?

Professor Crabbe is short, with a wide smile and warm brown eyes. He doesn't look like a professor—no white hair, no tiny glasses. Instead, he's wearing jeans and a button-down shirt, like what my dad wears to interview people for his stories. And he's young, like Miss Vogel.

"Hello." He offers me a hand to shake, which a teacher has never done before.

I take his hand and shake it the way my grandfather taught me: a strong squeeze and up-down, then I let go.

"We're late," Miss Vogel says. "Come on, I'll explain things later."

I follow them into the auditorium, where kids are fooling around on the stage. At first, I don't spot Nev and Max, but then I do, in a far corner, huddled together, looking at a piece of paper.

Miss Vogel tells everyone to take a seat in the auditorium — I choose one on an aisle, several rows back from the group, hoping no one will notice me — then she introduces Professor Crabbe.

"Professor Crabbe is here to help us block our acts more effectively, and to teach us about stage presence," she says. "We are going to run through the first half of the show, and he will help us as we go."

I tune her out. The first act takes the stage, and I watch some of the rehearsal from my seat. Professor Crabbe stops them once or twice, has people move their spots on the stage, direct their bodies toward the audience a little more. It makes a big difference.

Soon I get bored from sitting in the same spot. If I had my camera, I could at least shoot stuff. I creep out of my seat and move around the auditorium, observing different angles of the students waiting their turn to go on, more acts on stage, and Miss Vogel and Professor Crabbe. I pause to watch the kids who are acting out a scene from their favorite movie, sit through the Co'Mo'Shun Club doing their dance routine, and — after Miss Vogel yells at the group once or twice to keep the noise down — observe kids doing their homework in the seats while they wait. I should probably be doing the same thing.

I am in the shadows of the stage, toward the front, and I catch sight of Nev and Max, who sit together in the second row. They whisper and pass sheets of paper back and forth. Are they doing Spanish? A science lab? (*What do we have for science homework? I should check my planner. Did I write it down?*) Whatever they're doing, I'm not with them. And I won't be next year, either. A sharp pang goes through my heart. Why am I even here?

I stay to the edge of the room and cut through a row of seats until I get to my bag. I'm outta here. This is so stupid.

I don't know why Miss Vogel wanted me here, but now it kind of seems mean. Like, "This is what you would have been part of if your grades were good enough."

I turn my back to the stage and head toward the door.

"Let's take a break. Ten minutes," Miss Vogel calls. Immediately, the room gets louder.

"Hess! Wait!" Is it Nev again? Do I want to talk to her? I keep going, pretending I don't hear.

But as my hand touches the bar on the door, the person calls my name again and I realize it's Miss Vogel. I stop and turn. She and Professor Crabbe are hustling up the ramp, straight for me. Nev and Max follow, a few rows back.

"Sorry, Hess," she says, panting a little. "You don't have to stay here all day, but I wanted Professor Crabbe to talk to you for a few minutes."

Behind them, Nev and Max stop. They whisper to each other. I have to work really hard to tear my eyes away from them to Miss Vogel.

"Sure," I say.

Professor Crabbe pushes the door open. "Out here might be better," he says. "It's so loud in there."

I step into the hall. It's deserted. The late bus isn't for another half hour or so, and any kids who are still at school are supposed to be in an activity, club, sport, or rehearsal.

He turns and says something to Miss Vogel, still holding the door open, and then follows me. I lean against a bulletin board and he stays by the door.

"Hess, Cathy—er, Miss Vogel, showed me the video you made for your MK Nightshade project. I was really impressed."

Miss Vogel? How? And then I know: I'd told her what happened, and my YouChannel privacy settings are probably still set to public. But why does he care?

"Oh. Thanks. It was fun to work on," I respond.

He shakes his head. "I didn't phrase that well," he says. "It's good. It's really good. How did you make it?"

So I tell him—about the bathtub (my fingernails are still bluish), the puppet, the toy pirate ship, and the shoot.

"You did that all by yourself?"

I nod, shrug. "Yeah. That's how I do a lot of stuff. I also make movies with my friends." I tell him a little bit about *The Spy Who Bugged Me.* He listens, asks me questions about the software I use, and seems really into what I say. No one has really talked to me about my films like this before—like they matter.

I like that he's into it, but I kind of don't trust it.

"So," he says, when I've finished telling him about *Spy.* "Here's the thing. I teach at a college—Chestnut College—"

"My dad went there," I say.

"Oh, really? Okay, good. But I'm also a filmmaker. I do documentaries and indie films, kind of like what you do."

I'm skeptical.

"Real movies are made in Hollywood, not outside of Boston," I point out.

He laughs. "Real movies are made everywhere, thanks to technology. What kind of camera do you use?"

I reach for my bag, stop myself, and tell him. He nods.

"That's not a bad piece of equipment. Plenty of indie filmmakers use that and an external mic and make great movies. You can do some good work with what you have. You can tell some amazing stories."

"I can't do special effects," I say, thinking about the chase scene and the explosions that I had to take out. I cross my arms.

"Not all movies need those," he says. "They're fun to see, sure, but you don't need them to tell a good story. A good story stands on its own. Try going small-scale for your next project. Go for a good story. Forget fancy."

"Sure," I say, more to get out of this conversation than to agree with him. I don't get why Miss Vogel wanted me to talk with him at all. It's like he's on a different movie-planet from me.

"Check out my stuff," he says. He hands me a business card with a web address on it. "You'll see what I mean. I'll be at the next rehearsal if you want to talk more."

"Thanks." I take the card, stuff it in the back pocket of my jeans. I have no intention of coming back to rehearsal.

The auditorium door closes behind him.

Go for a good story. Forget fancy. His words echo in my brain, but they have no place to go. I couldn't go for a good story, even if I wanted to.

I don't have my camera.

I don't have my friends.

I don't have a chance of passing eighth grade.

My heart breaks into a million tiny pieces.

A FEW MINUTES LATER

"So what do you think?" I lift my head. I hadn't moved from my spot against the wall, and now Miss Vogel has appeared.

"He was nice, I guess." I shrug and stare at the floor. "Thanks for introducing me."

"You don't get it," she says. "He thinks you're talented. That you tell good stories." No teacher has said that to me about my work before.

Surprised, I bring my gaze up to hers.

"But that doesn't matter. I don't have my camera anymore." I fight tears and explain why.

Miss Vogel nods.

"You know that you can change that, right? Do the work and get your camera back?"

"I try!" I blurt. "Nothing turns out the way Ms. Walker wants, but still . . ."

"Have you been reading the book?"

I stare at the floor again, pick at a thread hanging from my bag.

"No."

‹‹ PAUSE ››

So this is all my fault. I know that, okay? But I'm so mad. I'm mad at Ms. Walker, my parents, and most of all I'm mad at myself. Why can't I be like Nev, or Max, or any other kid on the planet who does their homework and keeps stuff together? I'm so tired of being like this.

‹‹ RESUME PLAY ››

Miss Vogel frowns. "So you feel that you've worked hard, but—"

"Not for the right things." I cut her off, bitter. "Yeah. I know."

"That's not what I was going to say." She straightens, tucks a frizzy lock of hair behind her ear. Takes a breath.

"What I was going to say was, it just shows me that you're capable of doing great things when you are engaged and put your mind to it. Professor Crabbe agrees."

It's the same thing my mother said. *Ugh.* Like I should be able to flick a switch and all of a sudden be an awesome student. Like it's easy. Like it's just something I am refusing to do.

My emotions churn—anger, hopelessness, sadness, and back again. Miss Vogel watches me, waiting for me to say something, I guess.

In a movie, this is where I agree and we hug.

In a movie, this is where the main character leaves feeling better about herself, or at least like there's a solution.

I am a sucky main character.

"It doesn't work like that," I whisper, my fingers picking and twisting the backs of my hands. "I want it to, but it doesn't."

"But it *could*," Miss Vogel says. "Hess, you are the director of your own story. How do you want it to end?"

Huh. Her words fall into something inside of me, making sense in a way that nothing else has. Too surprised, I don't say anything.

She waits for a beat, then leaves me in the hall, alone.

End scene.

WEDNESDAY

Nev's mom gives me a ride to school. Nev is switching houses tonight, and she has her duffel bag and backpack—too much to carry when she walks.

"I wish you'd just stop this," her mom says in the same frustrated tone that my mother uses around homework issues. "It's been almost a year. Aren't you tired of lugging that thing around?"

"Nope," Nev says. "I choose not to divide *my* life."

Youch! I shift in the backseat, wishing I hadn't accepted their offer. Her mom's hands tighten on the steering wheel. But before she can say anything else, Nev twists around to me.

"Max and I have to work on our Hoot segment at lunch today. We'll be in the drama room, if you want to meet us there."

"Okay," I say, but I know I'm not going. Maybe I'll go to the library and work on that stupid fifth grade packet. It's like it's already happening—the pulling apart that will take place when they move on and I stay behind.

The car is in the drop-off zone. Nev throws her door open the second it stops, probably to avoid more conversation with her mom.

"Thanks Mrs.—*Ms.* Sodhi!" I call. I still haven't gotten used to her new-old name.

The second I step out of the car, my hands twist together and I force them into my pockets. Sarah will be in homeroom. Will I get in trouble? Will she know? What do I say?

"Gotta stash this," Nev says and heads to the office.

Alone, I drag my worry down the hall to my locker and homeroom. Sarah's not in her seat yet. I wait, stomach killing me, watching everyone who comes in. She doesn't show.

Something, at least, is going right for a change.

WEDNESDAY AFTERNOON

I'm at the kitchen table, papers stacked neatly across its surface. Mr. Sinclair asked all of my teachers to give him a list of what's due, and he sat with me while I copied everything into my planner and prioritized each assignment:

Wednesday Homework
Math sheet
Study English vocab words
Social studies questions
Write up science lab
Conjugate Spanish verbs

Mom and I have gone through my folders and organized them. Again. Now each one has two labels on the outside—one on each side of the folder, so I can grab it out of my bag and immediately know which one it is. We also put all the papers in the correct folders. This took a lot longer than it probably should have. It's almost six, and Mom hasn't started dinner.

"Can you get going on math while I make sure we don't starve?"

I nod and get the blue folder and take the worksheet out.

I make it through most of the problems on the front before my brain wants to take a break. I want my camera.

I get some water, sit back down, solve a few more problems.

"How's it going?" Mom asks, sliding chicken in the oven.

I mumble and finish the front of the worksheet.

There are word problems on the back.

Pat and Stacy want to open a business selling pens. Their goal is to have a 40% increase in profit next year. If their cost . . . The words blur. How am I supposed to do this? I'm taking summer school for math because I can't do it.

I squirm in my seat, try to focus.

If their cost per pen is .36 cents, and they sold 4,332 pens last year, how many pens do they have to sell this year?

"A lot," is what I want to write. But I don't. I copy the numbers onto some scrap paper, and make a table like the math teacher showed us, but I don't know where stuff goes in the table.

I divide the number of pens by the cost, but the number doesn't seem right. I put my head down. What is the use of all of this? I'm never going to sell pens or anything else.

"Having trouble?" Mom is at my elbow. I nod without lifting my head from my arms. I want to shout, *Yes! I'm having trouble. And there's still more to do when I'm done with this!* I'm so tired, I just want to lie down.

"Let's see." Mom loves word problems. I raise my head and watch her multiply to figure out how much money they made, then do some fancy division, and then I lose track because the garlicky smell of the roasting chicken and potatoes for dinner makes my stomach rumble.

"See?" She slides her scrap paper toward me. "I modeled it for you, so you can do the other one." Like I'm supposed to be able to figure out what all of her numbers mean.

"Thanks?" I stare at the paper.

"You don't follow," she says. I shake my head.

"Not even a little."

She sighs, points to each step, explains it. I still don't really get it, but she helps me with the other one so that's done.

And it's after six thirty and I still have so much stuff on my list and I want my camera and I really want the laptop so I can check out Professor Crabbe's website and movies.

And I can't have either right now.

I rub my eyes.

"Dinner will be ready in fifteen minutes," Mom says. "Why don't you take a break until then, and pick it up after we eat?"

She doesn't have to tell me twice. I draw a thick black line through *Math sheet* in my planner and push back from the table. With no camera, I have no plan.

"Clear your stuff?"

I scoop all of my books and papers together and put them back in my bag. Behind me, Mom sighs.

Sarah's right.

Mess: 1

Hess: 0

A FEW MINUTES LATER

After dropping my book bag on a pile of laundry next to my bed, I wander around the house, looking for something to do.

Dad's in his office, good hand buried in his spiky hair, staring at the computer. The only light in the room comes from his monitor. I flick the switch next to the door, and a yellow glow comes from the lamp on his desk. He jumps and spins the chair toward me.

"Hey!"

"Not good for your eyes," I say.

He gestures to the big chair in the corner with his bad elbow, and I curl up in it, feet tucked under my butt.

"How's it going?" he asks.

I shrug.

"You?"

He shrugs with one shoulder.

"I can't type one-handed, and I need to make the deadline on this article." He tells me more: It's the one about Nazari's Bakery. This time, I pay attention. He's got the ideas, but it's not coming across on the page. "I'm just too *slow*," he finishes. "I feel like I can't get it done."

I get that.

"Can I help?" I ask. "I can type pretty fast." It feels like a weird thing to do—offer a parent help like that. I mean, I'm used to setting the table or putting away groceries and doing chores, but this is helping in a different way. They're capable of doing those other chores, but so am I. Dad isn't capable of working right now.

Dad studies me, not saying anything. The computer hums, and the clinks and thunks of Mom setting the table reaches us.

"Why not?" he says finally.

We trade seats. I adjust his desk chair and he scoots the big chair closer to me.

"Okay," he says. "Read me what I've got so far."

"There's a new place in town, Nazari's Bakery. Owned by the Nazari family, this traditional Middle Eastern eatery offers a range of dishes as well as baked goods." It ends there. "Not bad."

"Thanks," Dad says.

"Is it a review of their food?"

"Kind of," Dad responds. "I want it to be a review and a way for people in the community to get to know the family. Okay, so . . ." He fishes through notes on his desk. "Here. Ready?"

"Yup."

"Okay . . . They offer pastries, light lunches, and catering for both home and office—wait, that's not how I want to say it."

I stop. Delete.

"Okay . . . catering for businesses and events." He pauses. So do I.

"No . . . that's not right. Go back to 'They offer pastries, light lunches, and catering.'" I *undo* back to that sentence. If he can't make

up his mind we will miss dinner for the next twenty years. I immediately feel bad for thinking that. This is hard for him.

"Have you tried any of the talk-to-type apps?" I ask, suddenly
remembering the one that Max has on his phone. He uses it to
record his awful commercial jingles sometimes.

"No." Dad's eyes brighten. "What're those?"

I grab his phone and do an app search. A whole bunch pop up.
I turn the screen toward him. "Read the reviews and download one
that you can also use on the computer. They're not perfect, but it
may help you go a little faster."

Dad takes the phone, studies the list. "This could be just what
I need. Thanks, honey."

I smile, glad to be able to offer a solution, not another problem,
for a change.

THURSDAY MORNING

Dad downloaded an app, but my never-ending list of homework kept me from my camera or the website. I'm tired and grouchy, so I keep my head down and my hoodie over my ears as I weave through the main hall to my locker. I miss my camera and want to be anywhere but here.

I twist the locker dial and prepare for the daily avalanche. As I wedge my shoulder in to stop the slide of papers, I catch hallway activity out of the corner of my eye. The rush of kids parts like a queen is headed my way.

It kind of is: Nev, on crutches.

I'm so shocked, I straighten and a wave of papers tumble to the floor.

I scramble to gather them so Nev's crutches won't slide out from under her, and when she reaches me I'm clutching them to my chest like they're plans for a top secret formula.

"What happened? Are you okay? Can I help you?" I can't seem to stop talking.

"Glass. Yes. Not with your hands full," she points out. I push everything into my locker, stuffing in leftover escapee math sheets and a social studies test (grade: C–). I slam the door shut, dimly aware that I've forgotten to take my books out for class, but whatever.

Nev's injured foot is wrapped in a bandage with her toes sticking out and covered in a plastic boot.

"Didn't you see my text? I dropped a glass on the bathroom floor at my dad's. Tried to step over it to get a broom, stepped *onto* it instead," she explains. "I need to stay off it for a week or so."

"I was doing homework and my phone died," I say. "Does it hurt? Why are you here?" I carefully slide her backpack off each arm as she shifts weight from crutch to crutch, standing on her good leg.

"I didn't want to be home," she says. "My dad was all stressed out and hovering over me, and Mom is in New York on business, so I can't go there. It doesn't hurt much. Just some stitches and glue."

I open Nev's locker—all of her books are neatly lined up by the order of classes and matching notebooks. She even has wallpaper and a glittery chandelier in there. My mom would be so impressed. As I reload her backpack, she leans against the lockers next to her.

"Crutches kill." She rubs an armpit.

"I'm so sorry, Nev," I say. There's an elephant in my throat. I struggle to find the right words to tell her why I really wasn't anywhere near my phone last night—why I haven't been anywhere near normal lately. They don't come.

"It's cool," she says, eyes down.

What does that mean? Is she mad? It's so hard to tell with her. Light sweat breaks out across my back.

She holds her arm out for her backpack.

"I got it," I say, probably too fast. The first bell rings. "I'll take it to homeroom for you. Max will carry it to your first class."

"Thanks," she says, "but you'll be late."

I shrug.

That's the least of my problems these days.

MORE THURSDAY

Nev's crutches make her a celebrity. Kids stop her in the hall and ask about her foot, and Max and I stand by, taking turns holding her backpack as she answers the same question a zillion times.

By lunch, she's over it.

"An anaconda nearly ripped it off," she tells a sixth grader. "It crawled up out of the sewer and through the bathtub drain." The kid scampers away with his cafeteria pizza like something is going to eat *him*.

Dark circles ring Nev's eyes. "I'm thinking that staying home and watching every Harry Potter movie ever made sounds good right now."

"At least it's Thursday," Max offers. "One more day and you can do that all weekend."

"Not the same," Nev says. "It's cheating when you do it on a weekend. You feel like you're getting away with something on a school day."

Max holds the bag of chips from my lunch. "Sour cream and chive! Sour cream and chive! Dixie's potato chips make you glad to feel alive!"

"That is just sad," I say. Nev nods solemnly.

"Really sad," she echoes.

"Speaking of the weekend, what are you guys up to?" I tread carefully but hopefully. "Want to do something?"

They exchange a glance. Max stuffs some of my chips into his mouth and busies himself studying the package.

"We're working on our Hoot skit," Nev answers casually. She takes a bite of sandwich. "But when that's done we can totally go back to *The Spy Who Bugged Me*."

"You've decided to do a skit? You didn't tell me."

"You didn't come to lunch yesterday," Nev points out.

Fair. I also haven't told *them* that my parents took my camera away. Because then I'd have to tell them why—and I just can't do that yet.

"Oh. Yeah. Can I help with the skit?" I cringe as I say the words out loud—they would have asked if they wanted me there, and seeing as how I blew them off last week, I'm sure they aren't going to go for it—but it's too late to take them back.

Nev looks at Max, who swallows. "Um, we kind of want to keep it a surprise?" he says, voice going up at the end like it's a question, not a statement. "We think it'll be more fun that way."

There's a hollow spot in my chest where my heart used to be.

"Oh. Totally," I croak out.

"Don't be mad," Nev says. "It's just a surprise."

No, it's "just" what next year will be like:

Me, alone.

THURSDAY EVENING

Tomorrow we have our last test on *The Giver*. I'm finally reading it, and it's not bad. The book is way better than the movie.

"Focus, Hess." Mom sits across the table from me, reviewing spreadsheets while I review the character list and story events from my notes. Well, that's what I'm supposed to be doing, but my brain keeps sliding to a zillion other things: how I'll tell Nev and Max that I'm failing, whether or not I'll ever get my camera back, why I should bother with this at all . . .

I've read Rosemary's description about fifteen times.

"Focus, schmokus," I mutter under my breath. I can't do it and I'm going to fail. Big-time. And there goes high school. And my friends. My skin gets tight and too-small-feeling. I tent the book on the table, lean my head back, and close my eyes.

Jack comes in and rummages through the fridge for a snack.

"What's that for?" he says. He grabs an apple and takes a loud bite. Mom sighs. I open one eye.

"Reading quiz," I say, more as a way to avoid the book than because I want to talk to him. "I can't remember anything in this book. It's going right through my brain."

"Story-design it," he says, spraying bits of apple.

"What?"

"Story-whatever you call it," he says. "You know, where you box out stuff for a film? Do it for that book, to help you keep it in your head."

"Storyboard." I correct him without thinking.

"Can't hurt," Mom says.

"Can I do that?"

"I dunno. *Can* you?"

I roll my eyes at him.

"Seriously. My calc teacher says that it doesn't matter how you get there, only that you get the material learned." He leaves the room, grabbing a banana on the way.

Mom looks thoughtful. "He's right, Hess. You should try it. You'll learn *something* by doing it, anyway. And . . ." She pauses, and her eyes seem a little watery behind her glasses. "And maybe we should try some strategies that make sense to you, not me."

Whoa. Not what I expected. I don't know what to say, so instead I pull out a blank sheet of paper and get to work.

I sketch out eight small boxes, then take a second sheet and make a character list. Next, I block out the big moments from the book: Jonas getting his assignment, his first meeting with The Giver, the apple—How would I have shown them differently in my film?

"Hess. Hess." Dad shakes my shoulder gently. There's a plate of baby carrots and hummus on the table near my elbow. Mom's seat is empty.

"Huh?" I grunt. He points to the clock.

I've been working on *The Giver* for almost an hour. The

storyboard is nearly finished, and it occurs to me that I actually understand the plot and message now.

Why didn't I think to do this sooner? Why didn't anyone think to tell me I *could* do this sooner?

"Gotta get ready for dinner," Dad says. "Clear off the table."

I stuff my work into a blue folder—social studies?—and crunch on a few carrots as I go. Jack comes through and grabs a handful, stuffing them into his mouth all at once.

"So gross!" I call at his back.

He turns and shows me a mouthful of chewed vegetable.

"Thank me later!"

FRIDAY

Ms. Walker passes out the tests, facedown. She pauses and her eyebrow twitches when she puts mine on my desk—or maybe it's my imagination.

Breathe: One-two-three-out.

"Do not turn your papers over until I finish distributing them."

My armpits are swampy with sweat. I squirm in my seat. In front of me, Sarah, with her sassy new pixie cut that everyone just *loves*, makes faces with Nirmal like nothing is happening.

One-two-three-in.

Ms. Walker stands at the front of the room. There's a softball in my throat and I just want to whip the test over and go already.

But she's drawing it out. Her eyes flick over each of us. She breathes in and out, like *she's* the one who needs to settle and prepare. Ugh.

"You may begin."

Twenty-three test sheets *shwick* over. Twenty-two pencils scratch.

I'm staring at my paper. The letters dance in front of me, floating above the page. I can't read it!

The ants crawl out of my socks. I'm going to lose it.

Close your eyes. Mr. Sinclair's voice comes into my head. *Don't let a piece of paper beat you.*

I squeeze my eyes shut. *One-two-three-in. One-two-three-out.*

"Are you all right, Hess?"

I don't open my eyes. I don't care.

"Fine," I respond. Her shoes click away one desk. Two. Three.

I take another breath, open my eyes.

The words pop into focus:

Match the name of the character to his/her role in the story.

One-two-three-out.

I can do this.

With each question, I feel better. A little more confident. The answers are there.

I blow through the test, the images from the storyboard popping into my head as I complete the ten questions. It's almost too easy. It's never been this easy.

Why has it never been this easy?

"Time." Ms. Walker comes down the aisles, collecting the papers. Immediately I get all panicky again.

"How was it?" she asks as I hand mine over.

I shrug. It's enough, but I don't want to let on. I am trying to keep the ants away.

She takes the pile, returns to her desk. We are supposed to read quietly, but I take out a notebook to work on *The Spy Who Bugged Me.* I can't concentrate; I'm so worried about the stupid test. Instead of making a shot checklist, I'm doodling boxes and question marks.

In a movie, this is where I would get up from my desk, go up to Ms. Walker, and have her correct my test in front of me. We'd high-five over the good grade, and I'd leave the class with a smirk on my face or a skip in my step.

But this is not a movie. I glance at her. Her head is down, she's twirling a green pen in her hair and frowning. Every vibe I'm getting is "stay away."

I squirm in my seat again. She looks up, through me.

I stay where I am.

LATER FRIDAY

I try not to spend the rest of the day thinking about the quiz, which is impossible. At lunch, I'm back in the library doing that lame packet Ms. Walker gave me, and I pass Nev and her crutches in the hall and she gives me a hard time for not eating with them in the drama room. My stomach hasn't stopped twisting since I turned the quiz in.

That's why, between fifth and sixth period, when I spot Ms. Walker coming down the hall, I prepare myself to be ignored again.

But instead of rushing right past me, she waves me down.

The test must have been so terrible that she came to pull me out of the rest of my classes for the day.

It must be so bad that I'm going back to seventh grade, never mind repeating eighth.

Before I can throw up on my shoes or run in the other direction, she has one hand out to stop me.

"Hester," she says. And I'm surprised that she can't see that I'm having a heart attack or coronary event or some other dramatic death-thing right in front of her. "Your test," she says.

The hall, filled with kids, goes silent. Pretty sure that my heart stops beating. Everything is in a state of suspended animation, and the colors are brighter: the storm cloud gray of the lockers, the dull yellowy off-white of the walls, and the electric orange, green, and pink flyers that hang all over the main corridor.

"I had to come find you. Oh! I should—" She cuts herself off. She's carrying a giant canvas bag, kind of like the ones that my mom puts eggplant and squash in at the grocery store, over one arm. She rummages through it.

If I were shooting this, it'd happen in slow motion to ramp up the tension. But I don't even need a camera trick. She must have six hundred papers in there, and she's looking at every single one of them before pulling mine out. It's like my locker is in her bag. I never understood what the expression "twisting in the wind" meant until right now, but I'll never roll my eyes again when my dad says it.

"Here!" She tugs a piece of paper, and my test appears like a rabbit out of a magician's (very cluttered) hat. "I'm really impressed," she says, and I stop listening.

There's a *90* at the top of the sheet. A NINETY.

I don't know whether to die of a heart attack or scream with joy.

I settle for tracing the numbers with a shaking finger.

"I will still be talking with your parents to come up with next steps, but it's amazing what a little hard work can do, eh?" She smiles, like this is some big joke. Like it hadn't occurred to me to do this before.

A shadow dims my ninety. "It was a *lot* of hard work. A whole lot."

"Well, good, then," she says, adjusting the bag on her shoulder. "This is what you need to learn, Hester: Doing the work is the most important thing. Tests show me who you are and what you're capable of. It's that simple."

When she says that, it's like a vacuum sucks the sunshine and joy from the world. And what fills the void?

Rage.

"You have no clue who I am and what I'm capable of," I say, unable to stop my mouth.

I take the paper, stuff it in my backpack, and walk away.

FRIDAY AFTERNOON

I walk home, heart as warm as the sun. In a movie, I'd go in and my parents would be in the kitchen, ready to celebrate my ninety. We'd sit at the table with mugs of coffee (them) and hot chocolate (me) and they'd gently tell me that even though I had to work extra hard, they love me and were proud of me. And there would be a family hug.

Instead, I go in and the kitchen is empty. So is the den, and Dad's office. A note is taped to the back of the front door.

Hess — Had to run out to meet w/ a client. Spoke to your teacher. We'll discuss when I get home. Jack at practice. xo, Dad

Ms. Walker's called? The joy of my ninety dims a notch or two.

I ditch my bag in my room. And then I'm standing outside of Dad's office. My camera is in the drawer under his printer. I saw it when he reloaded the paper tray.

No one's home. It's Friday; I am not doing any homework this afternoon. There's nothing for me to "focus" on. And them holding on to it is supposedly not a punishment, so . . . Before I can think too much more, I grab my camera from the drawer and head to the backyard.

Its weight is a comfort, and my eyes actually get a little teary when I turn it on. I know it's crazy, but I've really, really missed it. I pop open the screen and watch the images unfold as I shoot.

I wander around, getting up close with the shrubs, newly sprouting their leaves, the tulips and daffodils in Dad's flower bed, and capturing the way the sun beams over the fence. I try for different angles, better lighting. Zoom in. Pull back. Pan slowly. I have no plans to use it, no project to work on for school, nothing to prove. It's just me and the camera. I can take my time. Concentrate.

Why don't Ms. Walker and my parents get it? Why can't they see the difference between what I do with a camera and what I do at school? I don't have to finish an assignment by a certain time. Any checklists I make or marks that I have to hit are ones that I decide I need to do. All that matters is telling the story well or getting the image the way I want it to look—the way that's the most dramatic, or joyful, or just . . . cool. I can direct it the way I want.

SD CARD FULL

I sit back on my heels at the edge of the garden, replace the lens cap. When I turn around, Dad's leaning against the deck railing. I jump and try to hide the camera.

"I'm sorry, I know I shouldn't have . . . I just . . ."

"It's okay," Dad says. He smiles, but it looks a little sad at the edges. "You look so happy with it."

I don't know how to respond to that. "How long have you been there?"

"A few minutes," he says. He holds the back door open for me. A sense of dread creeps through me. What did Ms. Walker say to him?

One at a time, Dad gets two glasses down from the cabinet and fills them with ice and water while I return the camera to the drawer. He's getting better using his left hand, and doesn't spill a drop.

"Lemon?" he says when I come back in.

I shake my head no. He hands mine over. We sip and stare at each other. Dad's face is solemn, but he doesn't seem angry with me. His hazel eyes hold mine steadily, and although his hair is way more gray than the brown it used to be, he still has a young face.

"So," I say. And stop.

He puts his glass on the counter. "Your mom asked me to wait until she got home so we could all talk together. But I'm thrilled about your quiz score. Congratulations, Hess."

"Thanks," I say, heart full of light again. "The storyboarding worked so well. It was amazing. I can't believe I hadn't done that before. It was like everything was right in front of me."

Dad gives me a one-armed hug, then sips again, looks over the top of his glass at me.

"Hess," he says when he's done, "I want you to know something. Seriously."

Suddenly shy, I drop my eyes to the floor, which is fascinating.

"Hey," he says. He tilts my chin up to meet his gaze. "I'm proud of you. But not just for the test."

I misheard him.

"Huh?"

"I'm. Proud. Of. You," he repeats, slower this time. "Look, you did great on this one test, and not so well in your classes, but you've learned a lot this term." He cocks his head. "Haven't you?"

"Uhh." I do not think he means what Ms. Walker means when he talks about what I've learned.

"So look," he goes on, "no matter what happens with school, I want you to know that you're going to be fine. You're going to be fine as a grown-up. You're going to be fine as a teenager. School is important"—and he waves his hand like he's brushing dirt off the front of my jacket—"but it's not a measure of you as a person. How you handle yourself, how you treat people—that's what matters."

How have I treated people? Not well:

Nev—blown her off.

Max—lied to him and blown him off.

Sarah—gum. I wince.

Tears—just a few—threaten to slide down my cheeks. I don't deserve these words or his pride. He pulls me into a tight one-armed hug that smells like coffee and wet earth.

"Go download your footage and enjoy the camera for the weekend," he says into my hair. "I'm going to figure the software out and finish this project."

SATURDAY

I have my camera back for the weekend, and nothing to shoot. Normally, I'd do some shot lists and exterior footage for *The Spy Who Bugged Me*, but even that's not holding my attention.

Maybe that's because of the stuff I watched last night. I spent some time with the laptop, checking out Professor Crabbe's short documentaries. He did one about the residents of a local nursing home, one about the people who train to be rescue divers for the fire department, and one that focused on some jazz singer who I've never heard of. Aside from the boring educational films we watch in school, I'd never seen any movies like this. And I was kind of surprised by how much I liked them.

I walk around the house, carrying the camera, not finding anything except my dad, who is optimistically bringing out the stuff that we put away for the winter—even though it's still chilly most days. And even though he can only move things with one arm.

"Don't say anything," he says when he sees me coming. "I promise I'll stop when I get too tired." He sticks his good hand through the coiled hose at his feet. "And don't tell Mom."

I roll my eyes. "Fine." We both know Mom will find out and be annoyed. Or he'll overdo it . . . and Mom will find out and be annoyed.

"I was thinking," he says, after I help him move a bench that sits near our fire pit, "of going down to Nazari's to get some more details about what the place is like on a Saturday afternoon." He watches me out of the corner of his eye. "Any interest in joining me?"

"Sure," I say, although I'm more excited than I let on. "Let me get my stuff."

SATURDAY — NAZARI'S BAKERY

The bell over the door tinkles and immediately the warm, sweet smell of breads and treats hits my nose.

Zada's face brightens when she sees me, and I wave to let her know that I can see she's busy. Dad gets in line and I cross the room, past the café tables and chairs, and stand in the corner. I turn on my camera, sweeping it around the space.

INT. Nazari's Bakery. A crowded Saturday morning, people wait in line. Across the front of the bakery are the display cases. ZADA is behind the counter, refilling display trays, and MRS. NAZARI is at the register. MR. NAZARI boxes orders as fast as people can give them to him. There's a line of customers waiting for their turn.

MR. NAZARI closes a box and puts a sticker on it, then slides the box to his wife.

MR. NAZARI
Three tarts and a pre-sliced loaf!

MRS. NAZARI

That will be seven-fifty.

A man hands her cash; she makes change in the register.

Thank you.

MR. NAZARI

Next!

The bustle continues.

ZOOM IN: A display case of baklava, tarts, and cakes.

PAN TO: ZADA, filling the coffee machine. The clang of trays hitting the counter nearly drowns out the orders.

I don't want to get in the way, so I try to be mindful of where I'm standing. Two women a few people back from my dad in line are having a heated conversation about the baklava.

WOMAN #1

It's delicious. I don't know what your deal is, Peg.

WOMAN #2

I'm just saying they use too much honey. It's too sticky.

WOMAN #1

(rolls her eyes)

It's <u>supposed</u> to be sticky.

I shoot while they place their order, and then Zada comes into my frame. I click the camera off, close the lens cap. The rush has cleared out.

"I am on a break," she says. "Want to sit down?" She points to an empty table. Dad is speaking with Mr. Nazari off to one side of the counter.

I sit and Zada returns to the display case, opens a panel, and comes back with a big square of the sticky baklava on a plate with two forks.

I smile and raise my fork. Zada looks confused.

"Like a toast," I say, gesturing with the utensil. Her expression is confused, but she holds her fork up and I clink it with my own. She grins and we dig in. The honey-flavored syrup and minced nuts are just right. I don't know what Peg's deal is, either. This is ridiculously good.

"Did you like the books?" Zada asks quietly, like she's afraid I'm going to say no. I nod, mouth full. This stuff is a bear to get out of my braces, but I don't care.

"Loved them," I say after I swallow. "I brought them with me." I have them in my bag at my feet. I can't even believe I read two books this week.

"Can I see the movie you're making?" Zada says.

I cock my head at her. "Movie?" How does she know about *The Spy Who Bugged Me?*

"With your camera?" She points to it, sitting on the table. And then I get it.

"Oh, I'm not actually making a movie. Well, I am, but not this. I'm recording the shop to help my dad, since he can't take notes that well right now. He watches the footage and it helps him remember and write his story."

Disappointment flits across Zada's face. "I thought we were going to be in a movie."

"Well," I say, thinking fast, "I do have two days' worth of footage. There's no reason why I can't put something together for you." Running through a quick catalog in my mind, I realize that I have a lot of material for a "small story," like Professor Crabbe said to try—the interviews with her parents, the footage of the store, their apartment . . . It's enough material to make a short documentary, maybe.

"Let's keep it as a surprise," I say. "Do you want to help me work on it?"

"I'd love to," she says with a wide grin. "That would be awesome!"

And just like that, I have a new movie project. And helper.

THIS WEEK

SUNDAY EVENING

My weekend is not exactly a heartwarming comedy, but it's not a horror movie, either. Mom and Dad are happy with my ninety, but we "still have things to discuss." I don't think we do.

"School is important," Mom says, just like Dad. We're sitting in Dad's office. He's moved stacks of paper off the armchairs for Mom and me. "And we understand that we've had extenuating circumstances, Hess, but the extenuating circumstances of the last few weeks happened after this downward spiral had already begun."

I kick at the leg of the chair. Any reassurance I got from Dad on Friday is long gone. "I know."

"So you have to do better," Mom continues.

"I'm trying!" I wail. "You know I am. Dad knows I am. My brain is just broken." This is the way I'll be forever. Haven't they been listening? I pick at a thread on the seam on the chair.

"Stop that, Hess."

I stop.

"We know you're trying." Dad's turn. "And you're not broken. We just need to help you figure stuff out in a way that works for you. Which is why we want to run something by you. What if you had another chance?"

Ugh. Are they kidding?

"Staying back, you mean."

Mom and Dad shake their heads. "Not what we mean," Mom says.

"What's another chance, then?" I cross my arms.

"Summer school," Mom offers.

"It's not ideal," Dad says. "But we think it's the best option."

"Ms. Walker never said that was an option. I'm supposed to only take two summer courses, and I don't think I can get my math or social studies grades up."

"Well," Mom says, "when I spoke with her the other day, we discussed it. I explained how you tried storyboarding, and she appreciated that that helped you. Your test results backed that up. So Mr. Sinclair and I worked on a plan together. There are some . . . conditions that you have to meet to make it work."

"Conditions?"

Dad holds up one finger: "Do your reading for the term. Audiobooks or graphic novels are okay media for you to use. But you have to make time and do it."

Two fingers: "Achieve C minuses or higher on quizzes, papers, and projects. And set up private testing time *in advance* with Mr. Sinclair."

Three fingers: "Turn everything in on time."

Four fingers: "Continue to limit the camera to weekends and special projects only." That one stings.

"Do you think you can do that?" Mom asks.

Honestly, that list sounds like a very tall mountain to climb.

How can I do all of that *now* when I've been trying to do that all term and it hasn't worked? What if I can't? And how can I do *anything* without my camera?

"If I got C minuses for the rest of the term I'd be passing," I say, hoping to poke a hole in their idea.

"But your second trimester grade is not passing," Mom says quietly. "You need to pass third trimester so you can replace second with the summer session."

Oh.

"So in a way it's like starting over, with third trimester?"

"Kind of," Dad says.

"And I suppose there's not a situation where I could have unlimited access to my camera?"

Mom just raises her eyebrow at that one.

We sit. No one says anything. Dad's computer hums. Mom's phone beeps, but she doesn't look at it. I study the whirls in the rug.

"I don't know that I can do it," I whisper to the floor. My hands twist in my lap.

"You have help," Mom says.

"I had help all year. And we're still having this conversation."

"True," Dad says. "You have some new things to try," he adds.

"You have some choices to make," Mom adds.

Bits of white paper and lint dot the rug. No one has vacuumed in a while.

"What if I can't?" I say finally, the words painful.

"What if you can?" Dad retorts. "You *did* just get a ninety on a test."

I did. Doing it my way. And now, maybe, I can do more of that.

"I'll try," I whisper to the rug lint. Right now that's the best I can do.

☆　　☆　　☆

Mom and Dad finish with me, and I flee upstairs. I take out a notepad, flip past storyboards and scene notes, and find a fresh page.

(This shot of me working would be so cliché on screen.)

I split the sheet in half with a heavy line.

I write *What I have to do* at the top of one column and *Can I do it?* at the top of the other.

<u>What I have to do</u>
Read for the rest of the term (my way)
C— or higher on quizzes, papers & proj (set up extra
　　testing time)
Turn stuff in on time

I chew on the end of the pen, bounce the slick plastic off my teeth.

Can I do it?

In theory, I *can*. I mean, it's not going out and slaying a dragon, or moving to a new country not knowing the language —and having to go to school. But it's still hard.

The more I look at the list, the faster tiny doubt-voices creep in: How am I seriously going to do this? There's a lot to tackle. I can't even remember to get rid of the old fruit in my locker, let alone get this organized.

Crashing onto my bed, I flop my pillow over my face. How am I going to get out of this? My friends will probably think I deserve to stay back, my teachers probably don't think I can pull it off, and I will probably never get to take my camera to school again.

And—oh, yeah—I'm still failing eighth grade. And have to take summer school. No matter what I do.

Maybe I should just stay in bed forever?

I press the pillow tight and shout into it. It's not one of Mr. Sinclair's strategies, but it *is* satisfying. I do it again.

After two more lung-busters into the pillow, my insides feel empty and my head buzzes. That might be because I am lacking air.

I move the pillow and take a few cool, deep breaths. Stare at the ceiling.

Miss Vogel told me to be the director of my own story.

What kind of director am I?

That sparks something in me. I slide off the bed and reread my list. Everything that got me here has been about me: my choices, my decisions, and my actions. I haven't been thinking about any of those things like a director with an idea or a plot—only floating from mistake to mistake, bad choice to bad choice. This story would go nowhere.

How would I direct this story differently? Would I let this stuff happen again?

Do I wan... ...ff to happen again? Do I want to fail, over and over, with ... *ally* trying to change my story?

It's sca... ...hink about. Then I remember all the times I just didn't do what I was supposed to in class, or never checked the date of a test or an assignment. That stuff is pretty easy to change. Way easier than the stuff that Zada had to change.

I take a breath, and I write *yes* in the *Can I do it?* column.

I chew on the pen some more. Then I add something else to the list:

Read for the rest of the term (my way)
C– or higher on quizzes, papers & proj (set up extra
    testing time)
Turn stuff in on time
* Explain everything to Nev & Max
Can I do it?
I have to

I pause, and the weight of this sinks and seeps into me, heavy and important. There's no choice. They have to know what's going on, otherwise our friendship will be over before graduation. Hopefully it's not too late.

Then, in a flash of energy and ideas, I add one more thing to the list:

**Secret project
Can I do it?
You bet!!

Even though the list is long, now I don't feel discouraged. If I can do this stuff, I reason, everything changes. *I can change it.* It might not be easy, and I know it won't be perfect, but it can be *different.*

Across the top of the whole page, in big, block letters, I print:

I AM THE DIRECTOR OF MY OWN STORY.

I grab a thumbtack from my desk and stick the list on the back of my bedroom door. Folding my arms, I read it through again.

For once, I feel like taking charge, not like giving up.

For once, I don't feel like a failure.

For once, I think I might be able to pull it off.

MONDAY MORNING

I go to school early and find Ms. Walker in the teachers' prep room. She collects her photocopies and stacks them neatly. As soon as she sees me, she says, "Wait one second," and comes back with Mr. Sinclair.

We go into his office. Ms. Walker clutches her copies to her chest like they're her armor.

"Your mom and dad didn't come with you?" Mr. Sinclair asks. He points to the squashy red pillow chair that I fell asleep on a few days ago. I shake my head. It feels better to stand.

"I didn't want them to."

Ms. Walker tucks hair behind her ears. "Did they tell you what we talked about?"

I nod. "That's why I'm here. I want to let you know that I'm going to work really hard to do everything I have to so I can pass third marking period and go to summer school to make up for second. But I also want to ask you to do something for me."

Ms. Walker's eyebrows go up. "You want me to do something for you?" she repeats.

"Yeah." And I tell her and Mr. Sinclair what I need.

Mr. Sinclair's smile stretches as wide as a four-lane highway. Ms. Walker isn't smiling so much.

Okay, not at all.

"I'm afraid I can't do that," she says crisply.

Mr. Sinclair looks as shocked as I feel.

I breathe deep, pushing down the rising edge of panic threatening to knock me over. *Don't freak out*, I say to myself. *Don't freak out.* In the movies, here's where I'd make a passionate speech, and Mr. Sinclair would back me up.

"Why not?" The words squeak out of me, more chipmunk-style than passionate, but I'm grateful that they come.

"You're not academically eligible to participate in *any* extra-curricular activities," she says, hands on her hips. "It's not fair or possible."

Feathers would crash in this silence.

"I'm sorry," she adds. "It's the rule."

In a movie, I'd yell, "ALL YOU EVER CARE ABOUT ARE THE STUPID RULES. DON'T YOU SEE THAT PEOPLE CAN'T FIT INTO ONE-SIZE-FITS-ALL BOXES?" There might even be a dance number, where I'd whirl around the room à la *The Breakfast Club*, jump on the desk, and trash the joint to make a point.

Instead, my body shakes, tears well up in my eyes, and I struggle not to let them fall.

"Anything is possible," I say through gritted teeth. "If you try hard enough." It is one of Mr. Sinclair's favorite sayings. Do I see a flicker of a triumphant grin on his face? Maybe.

He hands me a late pass for first period. I take it a little too roughly.

And then I do whirl around.

And leave.

A FEW SECONDS LATER

If this were a movie, there'd be a montage. You'd see me studying, studying, studying. Maybe a shot of my camera, time-lapsing and getting dusty. Maybe some scenes of me getting C pluses or even a B minus on a quiz. You might even see me jumping for joy, or grinning. The soundtrack would be a driving, uplifting pop song.

That's not how this goes. Instead, I leave Mr. Sinclair's office discouraged and sad, wondering if making an effort is even worth it. Ms. Walker is waiting for me to make one wrong move, and then I'll be stuck in eighth grade next year.

Unlike what it says on my list, I probably can't talk to my friends about it. Nev and Max are really into finalizing their skit and living their normal, good-grade lives. I'm like a ship unmoored, floating around until something bumps me in a new direction.

Kids literally bump and nudge through the halls between classes. There's a tap on my shoulder. I turn, and there's Zada.

"Hi," she says, eyes down and a little pink in her cheeks.

"Hey," I say. We step out of the flow of traffic.

"You look sad," she says.

I debate lying. I am tired of lying. "I kind of am. Things aren't going well with my teachers."

"I'm sorry," she says. "Is there someone you can talk to? Someone who can . . ." She thinks for a second, maybe trying to come up with the right word. "Who can translate your problem for you?"

I'm about to brush off her idea, and then a bolt of electricity shoots through me.

"Zada! You're right. I need a translator. Thank you!" I give her a quick hug and race off to find the person who may be able to help me.

☆   ☆   ☆

Her back is to me, coming out of the second floor copy room with another pile of packets when I spot her.

"Miss Vogel!" I call. She stops, turns around. I rush up the hall, dodging kids. There isn't much time before the bell.

I skid up to her, panting, and before she can say anything, my mouth blurts out: "I have a small story movie that I want to show in the Hoot but Ms. Walker won't let me."

"Small story?"

"Professor Crabbe calls them that," I say, rushing through.

"And Ms. Walker won't let you participate because of your grades, correct?" she asks.

I nod.

"Can you talk to her? Please?"

Ms. Vogel's eyebrows nearly come together over her nose. She crosses her arms, which click with about a dozen bracelets.

The bell ending homeroom buzzes. The late pass in my pocket isn't worth anything now. And it looks like I'm totally sunk.

"I, uh, have to get to class."

"Listen, Hess. Is the movie finished?"

"Almost," I lie. "I need to do some editing." *Of the whole thing that I haven't really put together yet*, I add in my head.

"Well, maybe we can interpret 'academic eligibility' to mean that kids who are coming to rehearsal aren't using time when they should be studying to work on the show. Got it?" She waits for me to nod. "But if you are showing a film, there's nothing to rehearse . . . Do you understand?"

Slowly, I figure it out. "You're saying you'll let me enter the film even though I can't participate in the show."

She nods. "I don't believe in keeping a student away from something like this with the talent you have. It won't be eligible for a prize, but I want you to be able to share it with the community. Will you bring it to me when it's ready? I need to check the content," she says apologetically.

I can't even say anything, I'm so excited and grateful. For the first time, I can show Ms. Walker, my classmates, the teachers—everyone—what I'm good at. That even though grades and tests matter, that's not the whole picture.

Miss Vogel shoos me to class.

There might be a happy ending to this story, after all.

‹‹ PAUSE ››

Here's what it's like to actually put a movie together:

First you have to sit down with your raw footage. Most film-makers have an idea as to how much material they have when they're working on a project, but I've been shooting . . . well, forever. And when I actually look at my catalog, there's about eighty to one hundred hours of stuff shot at school: interviews, scenery, skits and projects, shots of teachers, plus the stuff from Nazari's . . . lots of it is worthless, but there are some gems.

Then you consult with your outline, or story arc. Every movie has one, and it comes from the script (or before the script is written). This way, you know the story you're trying to tell.

Thanks to Ms. Walker, I know exactly what story to tell.

Next it's a matter of organizing and editing the footage to fit the story. The storyboard shows you what the major moments should include and when, so you'll get the most emotional bang for your buck. Lastly, I load the raw footage into my editing software and piece it together.

« RESUME PLAY »

TUESDAY MORNING

Even though Mom and Dad won't give me my camera back during school hours, they agreed to let me edit and work on the project once my homework is done.

And, in keeping with my end of the bargain, I sit in each of my morning classes and try to pay attention. It's hard. So hard.

Especially when my mind wanders, or when I get bored. But then I remind myself of Mr. Sinclair's strategies:

A clear desk equals a clear mind, Hess.

A place for everything and everything in its place, Hess.

You need nets to catch information, Hess. Are your nets ready?

My nets are wide open. I write stuff down. I listen. I copy the homework assignments into my planner.

I even draw some of my notes, making storyboard boxes and stick figures and filling in information about the Industrial Revolution in social studies. It's not perfect, but it's better.

I'm not perfect. But I'm trying.

This is what it's like to try. This is what it's like to be the director of my own story, I tell myself.

When I see Nev and Max in the hall I want to tell them: I'm working hard. I'm trying to pass. I don't want to be left behind. But shame creeps out of my belly and instead I don't say anything. I don't even show up for lunch.

What if it's not good enough? What if I still fail?

MORE TUESDAY

I'm at a table in the library. I've finished my math homework and answered social studies questions. As a reward, I'm working on my new movie, coming up with some possibilities, when Max finds me at the end of the lunch period. He says, "Hey," and I gasp and jump about eight hundred feet.

"You scared the snot out of me!"

He grins a crazy grin and hands me a tissue.

"Ha-ha," I say. When the little joke is over, neither of us knows what to say.

Max shifts from foot to foot, frowning.

"What are you working on?" he says finally. "You didn't come to lunch yesterday or today."

I shrug. "Stuff." I don't want him to know about the movie, so I fold the notebook cover closed. "Language arts, mostly," I add quickly, because I'm afraid he'll leave if he thinks I'm being snarky. "What are you up to?"

"I need a book." He shrugs. "Social studies assignment."

"How's the skit going?"

"Uh, it's okay," he mumbles. He gets really interested in what's on the shelf next to me: bug books.

It feels like we're in a fight. Are we? I take a *one-two-three-in* breath.

"History books are that way," I point. My stomach clenches. I swallow, take a breath. I need to say something. But can I get past my word block?

"I messed up. I'm sorry."

It's not what I need to say, but it's a start.

He shrugs. "I don't know what we did, Hess. Are you even coming to the Hoot?"

His words sting. And then I realize: They think *I'm* mad at *them*? That is not good.

"Of course I'll be at the Hoot!" I sound annoyed, not upset. The helpless hole opens in my heart. I don't have the right words. Max sighs and pulls a book off the shelf.

"Really?" He kicks at the table leg with the toe of a blue sneaker. Wish I could zoom in on that.

"Why would I miss it?"

"Those two sixth graders sat our table today. They mashed up whatever was left of their food, stuffed it in a PowerDrink bottle, and dared each other to drink it," he says, changing the subject.

"Nasty."

"It grossed Nev out. I ate the rest of her sandwich." He tucks *Beetle Busters* under an arm. The bell rings. "If you'd been there, you could've gotten it on camera."

If I had a camera.

Before I can respond, he says, "See you."

"Thought you needed something for social studies?"

"I'm good." He brings the beetle book to Mrs. Coe's desk.

Telling my friends the truth might just be the hardest thing on my list.

TUESDAY NIGHT

"Eureka!" Dad bellows, scaring the daylights out of me. He races out of his office and through the kitchen and den. "Victory lap!"

Jack, Mom, and I, standing in the kitchen, stare openmouthed as he blows by, sling swinging.

"What is it?" Mom calls.

He races around one more time.

"I got it!" He's panting a little, eyes wide. "I got the speech-to-text software to work!"

"On your phone?" Jack asks. "Dude, I could've helped you with that."

"Not the phone, the computer," Dad says. "I can talk to it now and it will write for me. I got this!"

"You got this," I repeat.

He goes back to the office and his voice floats through the door. Mom shakes her head. "So glad he figured it out."

The Nazaris will be, too.

WEDNESDAY LUNCH

I admit it: I hide at the corner of the science wing and the main hall and watch Nev through the crowd at her locker before lunch. She's off her crutches but moving slow, and it takes her a minute or so to get her stuff switched out. She turns her head, as if looking for someone—Max? Me?—and then limps toward the caf.

My heart's hammering, and I breathe *one-two-three in*. I wish I could fast-forward through this part of my life.

I trudge to my locker, grab my lunch, and by the time I get to the caf the halls are nearly empty. My feet are weighed down, and I have to force myself to cross the room to our table.

I stand behind my seat awkwardly. No one looks at me.

"Um, can I sit?"

Max and Nev exchange a glance. Nev shrugs with one shoulder, and I know that I'm not going to be able to eat anything I brought.

At least Max will be happy.

I plop into the chair. Max has two apples, a bag of pretzels, and the remains of a sandwich spread out in front of him.

"Um, so," I say, and my throat tightens.

Nev, next to me, may as well be Iceman. Cold comes off her in clouds.

Be Black Widow. Miss Piggy . . . anyone! I remind myself. *One-two-three in.*

If this were a movie, I'd magically find the words. I'd say I was sorry, explain what's been going on, how weird I've felt. They'd listen quietly, be supportive, and tell me that they have my back, and we'd high-five or hug.

The words are hard to come by.

"Look," I begin. "I know I haven't been around. I'm sorry. It's just . . ." I stare at my unopened lunch and will myself to continue. "Things are kind of sucking right now." I pause and look up to see if they're paying any attention.

Nev has one eyebrow cocked. "Really?"

I really wish we weren't at a table, in the middle of the cafeteria, with sixth graders around.

I take another breath and fight the tears that appear in my eyes.

"Really. Like, Walker told my parents that I might not be going to high school next year if I can't get it together and I have been trying, and you guys are in the Hoot and I'm not, and it feels like it will when I'm held back and you're in high school, and my parents took my camera, but I made a new friend and she's cool!" The words shot out of me as fast as if the Flash pushed them. I'm surprised that it's over that fast.

And then my chest squeezes tight in reaction to what I just said. What are they going to think? Embarrassment, anxiety, fear . . . all three feelings churn through me. I can't look at them.

"Whoa," Nev says finally. "Hess, that's rough. Why didn't you *say* something?"

"Yeah," Max agrees through a mouthful. Pretzel sprays across the table. "Seriously."

"I just . . . didn't know how, I guess." I stop there. I could say that I was embarrassed, but that's embarrassing to even admit. I keep my eyes glued to the unopened lunch.

"We weren't trying to shut you out." Nev ducks her head to make eye contact with me, and I reluctantly meet her gaze. She's level, serious, concerned. The tightness in my chest loosens a little.

"We've just been busy with the Hoot." Max's words are clear now that he's not eating. "And honestly, it seemed like you hadn't wanted to talk to us much."

I nod, miserable. "I didn't. I felt like a loser. You guys are always helping me out with my work and stuff, and I don't do what I need to. I suck."

Nev blows air through her nose in a snort—it's her "give me a break" noise.

"You're only a loser if you don't let your friends help you when you need them. And if you aren't really trying when you don't let anyone help you."

Oh. Point taken.

"So don't be a loser anymore," Max says.

"I'll try not to." I swipe at my eyes with my napkin. Max takes my cucumber slices, and Nev elbows me in the side.

"And who's this new friend?" Nev asks.

"Zada," I say. "You'll really like her."

There's no group hug or high five, but a smile creeps across my face and I feel a little lighter.

« MONTAGE »

There's a frenzy of editing, tracking, and getting things just right. I'm just as stressed about this video as I am about failing eighth grade. Go figure.

I get my homework done at lunch. Nev and Max help keep me focused, and Zada meets me in the library during her English Language Learner period so we can work together.

I hunch over the laptop in the dark, during the day, in the morning. My brother tries to get it away from me, but Mom stops him.

"Let her finish," she tells him. She gives him her laptop so he can finish his homework. "It's important."

It's the first time I can remember that she has ever said what I am doing is important. She must see the surprise on my face, because she comes over and gives me a hug.

"You're not the only one who is trying to see things differently," she says.

« RESUME PLAY »

FRIDAY

I'm messing with the title, tweaking the placement on the screen, trying different fonts . . . as many teeny changes as I can make to get it just right. It has to be perfect.

"I think you're done." Dad's voice comes from behind me, and I jump. "Didn't mean to scare you."

"It's okay." I stretch and swivel in my desk chair to face him. He leans against the doorframe, and I tell him he can come in. He's not wearing his glasses, so his eyes look too tiny and squinty for his face.

"I do that, too," he says, and he sits on my bed and makes my stuffed platypus dance with a blue beanbag hippo.

"Do what?"

"Tinker," he says. The platypus dips the hippo. "I move words around, change them back, try again. That's how I know I'm done. I'm not making anything better, I'm just making it different. I can't get to perfect."

I think that over. The animals tango. "Yeah. I guess."

"You're done. Let yourself be finished." Hippo gets dipped one more time, then Platypus drops her.

He stands and leans over my shoulder. I get a whiff of

Dad-smell. When he sees the title, he smiles. His squinty, too-small eyes are just right.

"Just right," he says.

My guts twist. I'm not so sure about that.

"What about you?" I ask, saving the movie and closing the program. I'll drop it on a memory stick and bring it to Miss Vogel when I get to school.

"What do you mean?"

"Did you make your deadline?"

He nods. "We got the movie made, Hess."

We sure did.

FRIDAY LUNCH

I am way too nervous to eat. I left my memory stick with the movie on it on Miss Vogel's desk at the beginning of lunch, and now the thought of sitting in the caf, smelling today's special—tuna melts—does not appeal.

Zada is in the library, but I know I'm not going to be able to focus on my homework.

I need to do something that isn't going to get me in trouble.

To buy a little time while I figure that out, I head to my locker.

I spin the dial, then heave my shoulder into the space. And then I know exactly what I'm going to do. I slam the door shut and head down the hall in search of a giant garbage barrel. When I come across one that doesn't stink too bad, I grab its sticky handle and drag it up the hall.

This is it. I'm done with being Hess the Mess.

Twirl left, back around past zero, twirl right, then left again. I pop open the door and smoosh everything back in.

Then I purge. I grab handfuls of paper, scan the tops—science test from March, Spanish verbs from February, two science lab reports, a zillion notices—and pitch them. Out goes a very wrinkly apple. More papers. A green orange. I find a lip gloss tube with the top missing, and a bunch of language arts papers come out with an oily stain on them. The deeper I go, the more I uncover:

Flyers for the Christmas craft fair.

Social studies notes from November.

A zip-top plastic bag with a flat, moldy, green . . . sandwich? . . . in it.

And page after page of notes and papers. I'd be embarrassed if I weren't so mad at myself. How did things get so out of control?

A few tears come, and I let them. They are good tears, like I'm finally letting go of the Hess who couldn't make choices for herself. I even find a packet of tissues to wipe my eyes with.

I scoop and toss everything in the barrel, until the smooth metal bottom of my locker is visible.

Well, it's not actually smooth. There's some dark-colored, sticky gunk crusted on the left corner, but that's okay. I'm not perfect, either.

I stack my books neatly, my lunch on top of them. I even put the folders for my morning classes in there. My backpack is lighter when I pick it up. I drag the barrel to the other side of the hall and stand back to admire my neat, organized locker.

A low whistle makes me jump. It's Mr. Sinclair, who ninja'd himself right next to me while I was ogling my beautiful locker.

"Nice job, Hess! And good timing, too." He fans the locker violation ticket pad in front of me.

"It might not stay this way," I say, knowing that if I feel overwhelmed I won't be able to keep it up.

"It might not," he says. "But you can stop and fix it before it gets scary." He smiles.

I smile, too. My EFD might make keeping my locker neat extra hard, but that just means I have to work extra hard and fight the mess. I don't have to let it get this bad again. *I don't have to.*

That's not part of my story.

THE HOOT

A single spotlight shines on the stage. My stomach knots just looking at it. I'm so glad I'm in a regular uncomfortable seat with Zada next to me.

But I can't stop checking out the stage setup, deciding how I'd do it differently—the lights are too bright; they need a filter. The sign for the Hoot hangs too low in the back, so kids' heads will block it and shadows from the lights will stand out on it, which is a total distraction. Didn't Professor Crabbe help out with this stuff?

Miss Vogel steps into the spotlight. She squints.

"Welcome to the Howard Hoffer Hoot!"

People cheer so loud, my ears get a buzzy sound that I bet will hang around until tomorrow. It takes me a few seconds to realize that I'm screaming and clapping along with everyone else.

She waves her arms a bunch of times to get us to quiet down. Finally, we settle. Even though my movie is at the end, I'm on the edge of my seat.

She announces the first act, which is a lame skit put on by some sixth graders. Only their parents laugh.

Then come some routines by the Co'Mo'Shun Club. The whole time, Zada nods her head to the beat. The dancing is okay, but the sound guy has the speakers jacked way too loud and the music crackles.

"I liked that one," Zada whispers to me.

"I can tell," I whisper back.

I tune out for the next few acts. One of them is supposed to be funny, but it's just a bunch of guys spraying one another with squirty string and saying movie lines—half of which they get wrong.

(For the record, it's "Eat your food, Tina," not "Tina, here's your food.")

Lame.

Kids had to audition to get into this?

Then, Miss Vogel comes onto the stage and says, "Now for a word from our sponsor."

My body tingles, and I'm as nervous as if I were up there, too.

Nev comes onstage, dressed like that girl in white on the insurance commercial.

I want to throw up for her, but she gives everyone a smile. Her thick hair is out of her braid and held back with a giant blue headband. She winks at the crowd. She might actually be having fun.

She squints into the spotlight.

"Hey!" she calls to us. "Anyone out there?"

Max stumbles in, papers crammed into a notebook every which way, fly open, shoes untied.

"Me!" he yells back. "I need help!"

"What can I do for you?" she mimics the girl's voice perfectly. They didn't do any blocking, though, because Max keeps standing in front of her when they talk. They should be turned sideways to the audience, so we can see them both. I wonder if anyone is recording tonight? If they watched it, they could totally do better for tomorrow's show. I'll tell them later.

"I'm a mess," he says. A banana falls out of the piles he's carrying and it splats on the floor.

That's my bit!

And, come to think of it, so is the mess of papers he's holding.

And then it hits me: *Max is me.* He might not know it—they might not have intended it that way, or maybe they did—but it's me.

My face is so red and hot I worry that it's going to outshine the spotlight.

Does anyone else know? Does Zada?

"You need homework insurance!" Nev chirps. I want to punch her in the face.

She tells Max how affordable it is, what it does, and the kids around me are cracking up. "Sign me up!" someone yells.

"Me too!" another kid calls.

"Me too!" Zada pipes in.

More and more voices yell that they want in.

And it hits me: They need help, too.

No one thinks they have it all together, no matter how much they seem to.

Their skit gets the most laughs, and what's cool is that they come out two more times during the show and do different versions of it, like they're really commercials. I'm cheering with everyone else every time they come on stage.

Then, after an eighth grader who does a pretty good ventriloquist act, Miss Vogel comes back to the stage. Behind her, the crew pulls down the giant screen that we use for assemblies.

I had no idea they'd use that screen. I mean, it makes sense, but I've never seen any of my stuff on a screen larger than a laptop.

And all these people weren't in my room whenever I watched my own movies.

What if it stinks? I'm used to making big movies, action movies, nothing *real*.

What if I didn't write it well enough? Will it make sense?

What if no one gets it? Will they boo me?

My chest tightens. This was a terrible, terrible idea.

What was I thinking?

"We have a late addition to the Hoot," Miss Vogel says. "This student worked extra hard to put this together for our enjoyment. I think you'll be amazed and impressed."

Too late.

«« PAUSE »»

So this is where you came in, back at the beginning. Nothing is solved yet. Nothing is fixed or better or perfect. I have a lot of work to do on this story. Let's see how it ends.

‹‹ RESUME PLAY ››

I might puke.

Panic ants swarm my body. I can't sit here.

What if no one gets it? Will they boo me?

I scoot out of my row.

"Where are you going?" Zada asks as I pass her.

"Nervous," I mumble. I stand by the emergency exit door. A light breeze blows in around the frame. I breathe. Keep breathing.

"Hester? Is that you?"

Ms. Walker. She's leaning against the wall, a dim shape in the crowded auditorium.

"Hi."

"Did you . . . ?" She gestures at the screen.

My heart hammers, but I stand up straighter. "I did." I can't see her face clearly in the low light, but I'm sure she's frowning. My hands twist together.

The projector comes to life and the soft guitar builds through the overly loud speakers, and the title slides in from the top of the screen:

THIS IS WHO WE ARE

The song kicks in, driving, and there are the scenes of kids walking into the building, laughing, pointing. A close-up of someone's backpack. A shot of a girl dancing in the hall. Some guys playing basketball in gym class.

The words appear: *We aren't only what you see on the surface.*

Someone alone, writing in a journal.

The light through the cafeteria windows.

The sixth graders at our table.

Zada, wrapping her headscarf.

We aren't limited to check boxes and answer sheets.

Nev and Max, jostling each other because Max has snuck some of Nev's chips.

A bunch of rapid cuts of kids laughing. Looking serious. Concentrating. Studying. Running. In class. Working a fund-raising table. Zada at the bakery. Kids picking up garbage.

We are capable . . .

A sixth grader helping an elderly man with his basket on his way into the supermarket. Two kids hugging, one bleeding from a torn-up knee, a skateboard on the grass.

Of far more . . .

There's a picnic. A band concert. Play rehearsals. Sports teams winning and losing. A pair of girls holding hands. A boy practicing a speech.

I was able to get the audio and images perfectly in sync. Every small moment stands out like a tiny, sparkly gem. Somewhere, some part of me realizes that I made this. But I'm swept away, watching like everyone else.

Zada's ELL class, working hard. A girls' wheelchair basketball game. Sarah, with her pixie cut, helping a younger kid across the street. The images come faster and faster, piling on one another. And then, the final black screen:

Than you can possibly imagine.

The screen goes dark. My new production logo—a splayed banana with *A HessMess Job* written on the peel—appears.

My knees go weak, and I sag against the door.

It's done. It's over.

"Point taken," Ms. Walker says.

For what seems like a long, long time, no one makes a sound. Then one person claps.

And another.

And another.

And it's a roar, a sea of noise. Someone whistles. Someone cheers.

I did it.

‹‹ PAUSE ››

This is not a movie.

This is my life.

‹‹ RESUME PLAY ››

THE END

THE SPY WHO BUGGED ME (FINAL VERSION)

by Hess Greene

(edited by Bonnie Greene and Nev Chatterjee)

SUMMARY

AGENT SATCHEL must stop the deadly PROFESSOR D. STROYER before he runs his mind control experiments on teens, but MAXIMUM EVIL will do everything he can to foil AGENT SATCHEL's plans.

STARRING

Neveah Chatterjee as AGENT SATCHEL

Max Oliviera as MAXIMUM EVIL

Hester Greene as voice-overs for additional characters

CHARACTER LIST

AGENT SATCHEL: Super-secret agent. Works for Spy HQ. Smart, funny. Knows seven deadly martial arts. Carries a bag with hidden pockets filled with spy gadgets. Likes: sushi, puppies, tigers. Hates: bad guys, cows, octopi.

MAXIMUM EVIL: Bad guy. Works for PROFESSOR D. STROYER. Knows four deadly martial arts. Likes: kittens, pizza, soccer. Hates: secret agents, good guys, spiders.

ACT I
Scene 1

INTERIOR Spy HQ.

A quiet office. A desk, chair, clock, computer. AGENT SATCHEL sits at the computer, back to the camera, watching YouChannel videos of puppies playing. She is wearing a Spy Suit: black jacket and pants, hair wrapped in a tight bun.

Suddenly, an alert pops up on her screen.

ZOOM IN: Close-up on monitor, over her shoulder.

We read:

ALERT! ALERT! Professor D. Stroyer has taken a teaching job at a local school, hiding his true identity. He is planning mayhem and destruction, but we don't know what kind.

Your mission, Agent Satchel, is to sneak into the school, pretending to be a student, and find out what Stroyer is up to. When you find out, use your judgment and neutralize the threat.

This message will delete in four seconds.

A bomb emoji sizzles in the corner of the message. We see a countdown, hear a small pop, and the alert disappears. It's back to puppies.

AGENT SATCHEL
Adiós, Fido, Fifi, Frederico, and Franz.

She closes the window and puts the computer to sleep.

CLOSE-UP: AGENT SATCHEL's eyes, which are narrowed and angry.

AGENT SATCHEL
(voice-over)
I've got a job to do.

Scene 2

INT. School office.

AGENT SATCHEL, wearing kid-clothes, stands at a desk, talking to a SECRETARY who we can't see.

SECRETARY
(voice)
Here's your schedule, dear. I've asked one of our students to show you around today. You'll have math, English, science . . .

AGENT SATCHEL
(interrupting)
Is science with Mr. Stroyer?

SECRETARY
Of course it is, dear! He is our best teacher.

CLOSE-UP: AGENT SATCHEL's Angry Eyes.

AGENT SATCHEL
(in a low voice)
I bet he is.

Camera pulls back. STUDENT has entered the frame. This is MAXIMUM EVIL, but AGENT SATCHEL doesn't know that yet.

SECRETARY
Here he is! Max is also new, and he's fit right in.
Max, will you be our new student's guide?

MAXIMUM EVIL
(grinning at the camera)
Absolutely.

The two leave the office.

Scene 3

MONTAGE: AGENT SATCHEL sitting in math and English classes, looking bored. MAXIMUM EVIL meets her after each class and walks her to the next one. They look at each other suspiciously.

CUT TO: Outside of the science classroom.

AGENT SATCHEL
Thanks. I'm good.

MAXIMUM EVIL
I'm in this class, too.

They walk in together. A TEACHER is at the front of the room.

AGENT SATCHEL
That's not Mr. Stroyer!

MAXIMUM EVIL
We have a sub. Mr. Stroyer is . . . busy.

They sit at a desk. AGENT SATCHEL looks even more suspicious.

SUBSTITUTE TEACHER
Mr. Stroyer is working in Room 225 today, putting together something really special for all of you. So I'm covering for him.

AGENT SATCHEL
(to herself)
I have a bad feeling about this.

SERIES: Science class. AGENT SATCHEL keeps trying to get to the teacher's desk; MAXIMUM EVIL keeps bringing her attention back to him. AGENT SATCHEL finally succeeds in sneaking a piece of paper off the desk when MAXIMUM EVIL goes to the bathroom.

We see the paper: MIND CONTROL EXPERIMENTS ON TEENS, it reads in big red letters. AGENT SATCHEL is worried. She folds it and puts it in her notebook. Class resumes.

ACT II

Scene 1

INT. Noisy, busy middle school cafeteria.

AGENT SATCHEL stands at the edge of the room holding a lunch tray of lasagna, looking for a place to sit. MAXIMUM EVIL approaches, with a lunch bag.

MAXIMUM EVIL
Do you need somewhere to sit?

AGENT SATCHEL
(nods)

MAXIMUM EVIL

Follow me.

Camera follows the two of them. MAXIMUM EVIL leads her out of the cafeteria.

AGENT SATCHEL

(suspicious)

Aren't we supposed to eat in there?

MAXIMUM EVIL

(over his shoulder)

I have a better spot.

INT. Door to Room 225. AGENT SATCHEL knows what's behind that door. Her cover is blown.

AGENT SATCHEL

Hey!

MAXIMUM EVIL turns. AGENT SATCHEL tosses her lunch tray of lasagna right at his face. Takes off down the hall.

AGENT SATCHEL races down the hall, trying to get to the main office. MAXIMUM EVIL wipes his face, runs after her. Chase ensues. AGENT

SATCHEL throws hall garbage cans in his path. Garbage goes everywhere. MAXIMUM EVIL jumps over the garbage cans. He spots a custodian's cart, then he grabs a floor mop and throws it, like a javelin, at AGENT SATCHEL's feet. She trips and skids across the floor. MAXIMUM EVIL catches up to her.

They have landed right back outside Room 225. The door opens.

Scene 2

INT. Hallway floor outside of Room 225. The door opens, we see a pair of brown shoes and dark pants.

PROFESSOR D. STROYER
(voice-over)
I see you've found me. Come in, Agent Satchel. I've been expecting you.

MAXIMUM EVIL grabs AGENT SATCHEL's arm, leading her into the lab. Lab equipment covers the counters. There's a blue liquid in a beaker set aside from most of the equipment. We can tell it's important.

CUT TO: AGENT SATCHEL, tied to a chair. She is scowling, with Angry Eyes.

AGENT SATCHEL
You won't get away with this.

MAXIMUM EVIL
(leaning against the counter)
He already has.

PROFESSOR D. STROYER
(off camera)
Ready the serum, Max.

MAXIMUM EVIL pours the blue liquid from the beaker into a small glass, measuring carefully.

PROFESSOR D. STROYER
(continuing)
This mind control serum will make an entire population of teens ready to do my bidding. Their parents will be in danger. Their money will be mine. And I will have an army!

AGENT SATCHEL
(yawns)

All that's missing from that speech is a gleeful cackle. You are so lame.

PROFESSOR D. STROYER
(voice-over)
I am NOT lame!

AGENT SATCHEL
(shrugs)
Whatever. It's like bad spy movie writing.
Seriously, this is the best you can come up with?

PROFESSOR D. STROYER
(sputtering)
YOU are lame!

MAXIMUM EVIL finishes his measuring and has the blue serum in a small cup. He takes out a syringe and sucks the serum into it.

AGENT SATCHEL
You're not sticking me with that.

PROFESSOR D. STROYER
You're right. We're not.
(to MAX)
Proceed.

MAXIMUM EVIL steps forward with the syringe.

CLOSE-UP: It's not a needle at the end, but a hooked straw-type device. He's going to put it in AGENT SATCHEL's ear.

AGENT SATCHEL whips her head from side to side. With one arm trying to hold her head, and the other the syringe, MAXIMUM EVIL struggles. The syringe goes flying.

> **PROFESSOR D. STROYER**
> *(off camera)*
> You fool!

> **MAXIMUM EVIL**
> *(turning his back on AGENT SATCHEL to get the syringe)*
> You could help me instead of watching!

CUT TO: A shot of the back of AGENT SATCHEL's chair. She's been rubbing the tape around her wrists against a screw sticking out from the chair frame, and she breaks free. When MAXIMUM EVIL's back is turned, she reaches over to the lab equipment and throws the blue beaker of serum off camera, toward PROFESSOR D. STROYER. He howls.

MAXIMUM EVIL turns around. AGENT SATCHEL, her legs still taped to the chair at the ankles, is standing. She launches herself at MAXIMUM EVIL and takes him down, squirting the blue liquid in his face.

PROFESSOR D. STROYER AND MAXIMUM EVIL
(in unison, monotone voices)
What is your bidding?

AGENT SATCHEL
(grinning)
Sign my late pass and get me out of here.

ACT III
Scene 1

INT. Back in AGENT SATCHEL's office. Only this time, MAXIMUM is in there with her. We also see the brown shoes and dark pants of PROFESSOR D. STROYER. His body is off camera.

AGENT SATCHEL sits at her computer, watching the puppy video.

MAXIMUM EVIL
(looking over her shoulder)
They're so cute!

AGENT SATCHEL

I know, right?

PROFESSOR D. STROYER

(off camera)

May I look?

AGENT SATCHEL

Are you finished writing?

PROFESSOR D. STROYER

(silence)

CUT TO: A stack of papers on a small table. PROFESSOR D. STROYER's arm is in the shot, holding a pen. Written over and over on the papers are the words "I will use my scientific knowledge for good" in a numbered list. He's up to number 742.

PROFESSOR D. STROYER

Not yet.

AGENT SATCHEL

Then you may not.

(turns back to the puppy video)

Suddenly, an alert pops up on the screen.

ZOOM IN: Close-up on monitor, over their shoulders.

We read:

ALERT! ALERT! The evil Mr. Flee Bag is posing as a doctor at an animal hospital. He is planning mayhem and destruction, but we don't know what kind.

Your mission, Agent Satchel, is to sneak into the hospital with your team, pretending to be a vet tech and pet owners, and find out what Flee Bag is up to. When you find out, use your judgment and neutralize the threat.

This message will delete in four seconds.

A bomb emoji sizzles in the corner of the message. We see a countdown, hear a small pop, and the alert disappears. It's back to puppies.

AGENT SATCHEL
(to MAXIMUM EVIL)
Now that you're part of my team, you need a new name.

MAXIMUM EVIL
How about MAXIMUM GOOD?

AGENT SATCHEL
(nods)
Consider it done. Now, let's get to work.

AGENT SATCHEL and MAXIMUM GOOD high-five.

FADE TO BLACK.

TITLE CARD:
AGENT SATCHEL and MAXIMUM GOOD will return . . .

END

ACKNOWLEDGMENTS

Writing a novel takes almost as large a crew as making a movie does. I couldn't have told Hess's story without these amazing people supporting this book along the way:

My agent, Sally Harding, who patiently worked with me on getting this manuscript ready.

My editor, Erin Black, who took to Hess's story with enthusiasm and insight, providing invaluable feedback. Cover designer Mary Claire Cruz, production editor Rachel Gluckstern, and copyeditor Beka Wallin, for making sure the book looks good and reads well. Any errors are mine.

My critique group: Gary Crespo, Heather Hubbard, Wendy McDonald, Megan Mullin, Phoebe Sinclair, and Annette Trossello, who reviewed more drafts of this than I can count.

Technical advisors Stephanie Gorin and Ron DiRito, both of whom reviewed this manuscript with an eye toward film and video details. Mistakes and liberties are all mine.

Expert readers Penelope McDonald and Emma McDonald, for their help with authentic tween voice. And for help understanding EFD and how families work with that diagnosis: Kristen Wixted, Sarah Prineas, and Theo Prineas. Cheryl Klein, for championing this manuscript and offering excellent suggestions, advice, and feedback. Writing buddy Nancy Werlin, for providing unflagging encouragement every step of the way. And to Pam Scafati, who named the Hoot.

Finally, I cannot offer enough thanks and love for my husband, Frank, who manages everything while I write, and for Charlotte and Harker, who keep me laughing and always ask for stories. We got the movie made.

ABOUT THE AUTHOR

Erin Dionne is the author of five other books for kids, some of which are funny (such as *The Total Tragedy of a Girl Named Hamlet*), and some of which are mysteries/adventures (such as *Moxie and the Art of Rule Breaking*). Like Hess, Erin loves action movies, especially *Star Wars* and *The Avengers*. Wonder Woman is her favorite superhero. She lives outside Boston with her husband, two kids, and a very disgruntled dog. Visit her online at erindionne.com.

This book was edited by Cheryl Klein and Erin Black and designed by Mary Claire Cruz. The production was supervised by Rachel Gluckstern. The text was set in Adobe Calson Pro and Rockwell, with display type set in KG Next to Me Solid. The book was printed and bound at LSC Communications in Crawfordsville, Indiana. The manufacturing was supervised by Angelique Browne.